xmas '98

```
D1282457
```

The Flight of
the Osprey

The Flight of the Osprey

Ewan Clarkson

St. Martin's Press ⧓ New York

Library of Congress Cataloging-in-Publication Data

Clarkson, Ewan.
The flight of the osprey / by Ewan Clarkson.
p.   cm.
ISBN 0-312-13973-X
1. Human-animal relationships—England—Fiction.
2. Widows—England—Fiction.   3. Women—
England—Fiction.   4. Osprey—Fiction.
I. Title.
PR6053.L36F55   1996
823'.914—dc20   95-45791   CIP

First published in Great Britain by Judy Piatkus
(Publishers) Ltd.

First U.S. Edition: February 1996
10   9   8   7   6   5   4   3   2   1

To G. F. C. Of treasured memory.

The Flight of
the Osprey

PROLOGUE

Somewhere an owl called, the sound unnaturally loud in the stillness. Startled, a bullock galloped away stiff tailed across the meadow, leaving swirls of mist writhing and twisting in its wake. The watcher under the trees held his breath, and then exhaled in a long, inaudible sigh. His heart hammered, and his knees trembled as he struggled to regain his composure. He longed for the comfort of a smoke, but he knew that if Ernie saw so much as a glimmer of a light, or caught a whiff of smoke, he would use him as a punchbag.

Ernie reckoned he could smell tobacco smoke from forty yards away, and if he could, then so could the bailiffs. So he had imposed the ban, enforcing it on one occasion until the boy's lips were so swollen he couldn't hold a cigarette between them for a week. The man shivered at the thought, brushed away a mosquito, and then risked a glance at his watch. Two hours had passed. The gang had had time to net every pool on this stretch of the river by now. What was holding them back?

The night air was growing cold. Summer was passing, and soon the rains of autumn would bring an end to these forays. It would be time to turn their attention to the pheasants, or better still, deer. The demand for venison was rising, and one lucky shot would keep them in beer money for a week. Or put them in jail, or hospital even, now that the keepers were employing ex-Commandos and SAS men to guard the game. He wondered, not for the first time, whether he was not getting too old for these capers.

The growl of a diesel engine, driven in low gear, woke him

1

from his reverie. It seemed to come from across the river, but he could see no lights. It could mean only one thing. Next moment he saw three figures stumbling towards him through the mist, the bulk of Ernie's torso in the lead. He leapt into the van, stolen only hours ago, praying that the engine would fire, and let in the clutch as the others climbed aboard.

Not until they had safely negotiated the narrow Devon lanes, reached the safety of the motorway and were heading north, the speedometer hovering just below the legal maximum, did he dare to ask what had happened. Ernie let out an oath. He was wet to the waist, and sullen with anger. 'The net snagged. We've been all this time trying to get it free. Bastards must have sunk a tree stump or something on purpose to stop us netting. There was never anything there before. Now we've lost the net, and nothing to show for a night's work.'

'Did they see you?'

Ernie shook his head. 'Na. We were gone before the Landrover was halfway across the field. Too idle to walk. That's their trouble. If they'd come up the river on foot they would have fallen over us for sure. Now they won't even find the net.'

The lights of the service station loomed ahead. The van turned off the motorway and came to rest in a deserted corner of the park. The men dispersed to find their own vehicles, leaving the van for the authorities to find in the morning, a soaking wet passenger seat the only sign of its previous occupancy.

Beside the river the lone driver of the Landrover cast a long line as he worked his fly across the waters of the pool. He had come to fish for sea trout, a fish so wary and shy that it was almost impossible even to approach in broad daylight, let alone deceive with a lure, unless the water was discoloured by a flood. Even after dark they were easily scared, so he had been careful not to let his headlights shine on the pool. He was completely unaware that his stealthy arrival had put a gang of poachers to flight, or that below him an illegal net lay stretched halfway across the pool.

Two hours later, cold, and tired, he decided to call it a night. He had not touched a fish all evening, but he knew from long experience that this was often the way with sea trout. His leg ached abominably, and not for the first time he cursed the stray bullet that had caught him in the thigh. On indefinite sick leave from the army, he knew that it was only a question of time before a medical board downgraded him to a desk job. It was not his idea of soldiering, and he had already decided that when the time came he would resign his commission, and then perhaps he could come to live permanently here in Devon, close to the wild river he loved so much.

The fish could wait for another night. Right now he wanted a whisky and a hot bath. He started up the Landrover and drove away. The net remained behind, a silent, invisible menace to every fish that swam up river through the pool. The nylon monofilament from which the mesh was woven was virtually indestructible, and it would continue to catch fish until it was accidentally discovered, or a spate washed it away.

Chapter One

The rain sweeping across the forest carried the kiss of ice, and the distant peak of Ben Nor was capped with white. The great bird crouched lower in the shallow cup of the nest, her eyes half closed, her head drooping as she shielded the two eggs that lay snug and secure between her thighs and chest. Nine days had passed since the first one was laid. The second was just a week old. Another month would go by before the first fledgling chick broke from its shell, and spring, in the Highlands of Scotland, could be unpredictable, savage storms of rain, hail or snow alternating with blazing sunshine, days of suffocating heat followed by nights of hard frost. Throughout that time the bodies of the parent birds provided a living mantle, the only safeguard against a fatal chill from exposure.

From far away across the carpet of rain-soaked pine trees that mantled the sodden earth came a clear, high-pitched whistle. Seconds later the male bird swept into view, his wings outstretched, a fresh caught trout gripped in one scaly claw. He circled the nest and came to rest on a nearby tree, a pine long dead, its white, skeletal branches devoid of bark. Here he began to feed, leisurely tearing the flesh from the front half of the fish with his powerful hooked bill, and seemingly oblivious to the increasingly petulant calls of the female to be fed. At length, appearing to notice her for the first time, he picked up the remains of the trout in the claws of one foot and flew over to the nest, landing awkwardly on the rim of the great untidy pile of sticks and branches. The female hissed a greeting, glaring at him with brilliant yellow eyes, and then, abandoning her eggs, she seized his offering of fish and flew off to the perching tree to feed. Gingerly, the male took her place on the eggs, easing himself down until they settled comfortably against his flanks.

Ospreys had nested in the British Isles since the passing of the ice age. Gradually, with the growth of civilisation, their numbers had dwindled, their territories shrinking with the spread of man until only the most isolated mountainous regions provided a safe refuge for them to mate and raise their young. By the end of the nineteenth century even the high hills failed to offer the ospreys sanctuary from poison, trap and gun, so that by the beginning of the First World War the osprey was extinct in Britain as a breeding bird.

Then, after an absence of almost half a century, migrant birds from Scandinavia began to reclaim their ancient territories in the Scottish Highlands. By now the attitude of the human population towards these large, fish-eating hawks had changed, and instead of reaching for the poison and the gun, people grabbed their cameras and binoculars, and as news of the nesting birds spread, bird watchers flocked to the locality in such numbers that the birds were now in danger of being loved to death.

The ospreys faced further threats to their existence. There were some, riparian owners and fishermen, who were so set in their ways that they still saw the birds as a danger to their jealously guarded fisheries. However, these individuals represented only a tiny minority of anglers. Most were as delighted by the return of the osprey as they were to see an increase in the number of otters. Now the chief danger lay in the depredations of egg collectors, men who were prepared to pay considerable sums to possess a clutch of the rare eggs with their rich russet red markings.

So the Royal Society For The Protection Of Birds mounted a constant guard over the original nest site at Loch Garten, and rather than try to conceal the site from friend and foe alike, with considerable foresight they actively encouraged visitors and gave the nesting pair maximum publicity. As the years passed the fame of the ospreys and the visitors centre grew. Meantime, far from the glare of publicity in remote glens elsewhere in the highlands, sixty other pairs raised their young, the secret of their whereabouts guarded by wardens and residents alike.

The female tearing at the trout was one of such a pair. They had chosen their nest site well, in a hidden glen far from any road. A dense forest of ancient trees crowded down to the shores of a tiny loch, visible only from the air, and the hills around were deserted except for the ubiquitous sheep and a small herd of red deer. Few people knew of its existence, and of those that did, even fewer were aware of the presence of the birds.

The rain had stopped now, and a thin sun slanted down through the scudding clouds, transforming the moisture on the bird's plumage into a pearly iridescence. As if aware of it for the first time, she shook herself vigorously, sending a rainbow shower of spray into the surrounding air, and fell to preening herself, running each flight feather though her beak in turn. She was a large bird, almost two feet in length from head to tail, with a wingspan of over five feet. The feathers on her back and wings were a mottled brown, her chest and flanks pale cream, with a distinctive brown bar across her breast. Another dark stripe framed her lustrous yellow eye, and she wore a cap of brown which could be raised in a crest when she was agitated or disturbed. Her legs were green and sturdy, her feet perfectly adapted for fishing. Each was equipped with four long black talons, the points needle sharp. On each foot the outer toe was reversible, allowing her to grip her slippery prey with two talons forward and two back. To help her hold a fish the undersides of her feet were clad in scaly, prickly skin. Her great hook of a beak was strong and black, ideally suited for tearing the skin and flesh of her prey. Indeed, so successful were the ospreys as fish-eating hawks that their specialised way of life had remained unchanged throughout the millennia, and their populations circled the globe, wherever there were rivers that flowed, and lakes where there were fish to be caught. Only the activities of man caused any serious threat to their welfare.

Her toilet arranged to her satisfaction, the osprey rested

7

for a while, dozing in the faint warmth of the sun. Then abruptly she spread her wings and launched herself from her perch. From the nest the male called to her, but she ignored him and flew off, circling in slow, lazy sweeps, climbing ever higher into the sky. There were trout in the loch. She could see their long, sinuous shapes just below the surface, faint shadows against the bed of sand that lay below, but they were poor, undersized fish, their growth stunted by lack of food and the acid water that welled from the peat. In any case she had no interest in fishing at the moment. Instead she was content to rely on her mate in his role as the hunter and provider.

The skies around her were empty of life. A few hinds grazed on the hill beneath her, and a black-throated diver patrolled the far end of the loch, his mournful wail echoing around the glen. For a while the osprey gave her whole being to the sensation of flying, to the soft buffeting and gentle lift of the wind, the rush of cool air over her pinions, and the effortless ease with which she climbed. Gradually though, anxiety for the welfare of her eggs tempered her desire for freedom and she turned, closed her wings and fell, arrowing through the clear air in a shallow dive towards the nest site.

She did not immediately join her mate. Instead she pitched in the crown of a pine some fifty yards away, and here she used her beak to tear a small green spray from the branch on which she perched. Then, carrying the sprig in her bill, she flew across to the nest and landed on the rim. The male needed no persuasion to leave the eggs, and she settled in his place before carefully arranging the spray of pine needles just inside the rim of the nest. Other fragments of vegetation littered the nest, some wilting, some withered and dead. No one knew why the ospreys had this habit of decorating the nest, but it had been their custom from time immemorial.

Time passed uneventfully, long days when the sun shone warm and the loch lay like an emerald stone dropped on a carpet of moss-green velvet, nights when the stars sparkled with frost fire and white hoar rimed the nest in the early dawn. There were days when the wind blew warm and wet, gusting from the west so that the great unwieldy platform of sticks and branches twisted and groaned under the bird and her eggs. The pair had done their work well, however, and the structure held firm. Each morning the male bird brought fish to the waiting hen, and again in the evenings. Occasionally a buzzard, or more rarely an eagle strayed into their air space, to be seen off by the watchful male. Once a fox foraged round the base of the nest tree, and narrowly escaped being scalped. A wild cat had her litter of kits beneath a tumbled heap of boulders by the shores of the loch, but she hunted at night, and posed no threat to the birds. Then one morning, when the eggs had but a week to hatch, the stranger appeared.

He was called Iasgair, which means fisherman, and he was not quite two years old. The ring he wore on his left leg identified him as one of the young hatched in an eyrie fifteen miles away to the west. He had successfully completed his first migration to the south, spending two winters and a summer haunting the shores of a muddy estuary in Senegal. Now, though still too young to be a breeding bird, he had returned to his birthplace. Already, ospreys were beginning to be victims of their own success. As their numbers increased, as each new breeding pair colonised a new locality, claiming the territory for their own, so suitable habitats became harder to find. Often one territory overlapped another, and each was so jealously guarded by the occupants that they would brook no interference from strangers. So the young osprey found himself harried from one area to another. Luckily the Highlands of Scotland were vast in extent, the rivers and lochs numerous, and the fish stocks still fairly prolific. So in that second summer of his life the young bird lived the life of a gipsy, a vagabond of the skies.

It was perhaps a course in further education. Two years ago he had learned to fly, and although this had been partly instinctive there were degrees of skill he had to master before he became proficient. Then he had had to learn to fish and catch food. This had been even more arduous and demanding, as time after time his slippery prey had eluded him, but here hunger had been the spur that had goaded him on to success. Then followed the long journey over land and sea to West Africa, and his equally arduous return.

9

All this though was now behind him. Now he was studying sociology, discovering the whereabouts of his kind, gaining an intimate knowledge of his terrain, and identifying those regions in which he was unwelcome. The untidy conglomerations of sticks and branches with which the ospreys formed their eyries were so large and bulky that they were clearly visible, even from a height of a thousand feet. It was as if the builders wished to advertise their presence to others, and indeed there may have been some evolutionary advantage in this, the presence of a number of nests indicating good fishing grounds, which all might share. Nonetheless, the nest site remained sacrosanct to the breeding pair, and was best avoided.

Iasgair knew this, yet each time he located a nest site he felt drawn by some overwhelming compunction to take a closer look, even though he knew from experience that his reception would be hostile. Today was no exception, and he circled warily, his eye scanning the scene below, the shimmering loch, the dark carpet of the forest, the whitish sunbleached pile of sticks that formed the nest, the dark brooding form of the female at its centre. Somewhere, he knew, there was a perching tree, with possibly a watchful mate, but the only pine that looked at all suitable was deserted.

He dropped lower, until he could see the yellow eye of the hen bird cocked skyward, watching him as he made his descent. She began to scream, the crest of feathers on her head raised in outrage at his approach, but she did not move off the eggs. Iasgair swooped low over the nest, a mere foot above the sitting bird, who hissed and crouched as he swept past. He was climbing and turning, about to make another pass, when the male bird came out of the sun.

He heard the thudding beat of the aggressor's wings, the whistle of air through pinions, and felt the wind of their passage overhead. Razor-sharp talons hissed by his head and he dived just in time to avoid being decapitated. As it was he felt a violent blow on his rump, and a few feathers exploded around him. He did not linger to dispute the issue. Instead he folded his wings, and, like an arrow falling, plunged towards the surface of the loch. Then, his wings almost touching the water, he raced for the far shore of the loch. Honour vindicated, his pursuer followed at a discreet distance, and when he saw the interloper had no intention of returning, he broke off the pursuit, returning in triumph to the nest.

Iasgair flew on, climbing the hills to the north. Green slopes, the turf cropped short by generations of sheep, rabbits and deer, gave way to stony scree and crumbling walls of rock. Beyond the crest of a shoulder joining two peaks lay a hidden valley, the birthplace of a glacier that had once carved its ponderous way to the west. Here lay another small loch, its clear waters calm and mirror bright in the morning sun. Though its shores were barren and windswept, the bed of the loch lay on limestone rock, and in the cold mineral-rich waters life teemed. In the sun-warmed shallows weed grew green and lush. Snails and caddis grubs, shrimps and the larvae of mayfly and stonefly, infant fish and the tadpoles of toads and frogs, all provided rich feeding for the trout that prowled like hungry wolves.

A fish of about half a pound in weight lay basking near the surface. Iasgair hovered briefly, closed his wings, and dropped in a slanting dive. Both legs extended, talons spread wide, he barely skimmed the surface of the water, but in that instant his feet struck forward, gripping the trout across the middle of its back. Scarcely checking his flight he shook himself and sailed on, the trout still flapping in his claws, spray dripping in a rainbow shower. Iasgair shifted his grip so that the trout lay head forward, thus reducing wind resistance, and bore his prize to a rocky crag high on the mountainside. Here he dined, and then drowsed the rest of the day away, forgetting about his earlier humiliation.

Chapter Two

Spring merged imperceptibly with summer. At first the weather was unpredictable, fey, with icy winds from the north bringing squalls of rain, snow, and sleet. Then the sun would shine once more, bringing clouds of mosquitoes which drove the red deer higher up the hill, hoping to find relief from their blood-sucking stings in the cool winds that blew among the peaks. In the osprey eyrie the eggs hatched, and the young, at first helpless bundles of brown and buff down, grew apace on fish brought by the male.

His hunting success varied with the weather. On good days he returned to the nest every hour or so, six or seven times a day, bearing a fresh caught trout, perch, or infant pike flapping in his claws. On days when the rain drove the fish down, or high winds ruffled the surface of the water, making the fish difficult to see, he was not so successful. Always, he ensured that his needs were satisfied first, and at times he would devour three parts of a trout in full view of the nest, leisurely stripping the flesh from the bones, and oblivious to the outraged cries of his mate and the plaintive calls of the chicks.

The female was invariably the last to be fed, for the demands of the chicks came first, and so she was frequently hungry. Though this regime seemed harsh, it was essential to survival. The male had to stay in the peak of condition if he was to support the brood. The chicks needed food for growth, but the female hunted little, and so expended least energy.

By the beginning of July the weather set fair. A long succession of hot windless days followed, when the sun

12

blazed down and the female stood panting over her young, her outstretched wings shading them from the heat. Night brought some relief, but the periods of darkness were brief, and the days long. Now there were plenty of fish, more than the young could eat, and the nest grew foul with rotting fragments of flesh and skin. Blowflies buzzed incessantly round the remains, irritating the young and waking them from sleep.

Now the male hunted further afield and each day, in addition to the lochs scattered among the hills, he visited the broad river that flowed north through the valley. During the long days of drought the level of the river had fallen, and it now ran low and clear over the stones. The trout were fat with summer feeding, and he rarely failed to make a kill. From time to time he met Iasgair, the stranger, but he paid no heed to the other's presence on the hunting grounds. It was a different matter at the nest site, so although Iasgair lingered in the vicinity, and from time to time, driven by an intense curiosity, passed over the eyrie, he did not venture too near. Yet both birds continued to fish the river, at times so near to each other that on occasions they were mistaken for a breeding pair.

At one point the river flowed alongside the road, and passers-by frequently saw him flying slowly up river, hovering from time to time over the water, and sometimes, if they were lucky, they would see him dive on a fish. Further upstream there was a bridge, and this was a favourite vantage point for osprey watchers. Just above the bridge a power line crossed the river, and in order to make it more visible to ospreys, and other birds which haunted the river, red and white plastic strips had been hung at intervals along its length.

As the long fine spell continued, so the days grew hotter, and even the nights brought little relief. There came a day when the sun shone with a brassy glare. The flies seemed more active than ever, and the young ospreys panted in the heat. Towards afternoon dark clouds began to mass over the hills, a thin breeze stirred the leaves, and a cock pheasant crowed somewhere down in the valley. Lightning flickered over the jagged peaks to the north, thunder muttered, and a few drops of rain fell.

At sunset the storm broke in full fury. A gale of wind swept before it, threatening to tip the eyrie and its precious cargo down on to the forest floor. The mass held firm, however, but mother and young were soaked with the rain. Over an inch fell in an hour, and dried up streams became foaming torrents, racing down the hillsides carrying with them a flotsam of dead twigs, dried heather, bracken and leaves. At the height of the storm lightning struck one of the poles that carried the power cable across the river, cutting off the electricity to a number of homes.

By dawn the skies had cleared. A fresh breeze blew from the west, and the river flowed swiftly, its waters swollen and turbid with silt. At first light the power company replaced the damaged cable with a temporary line, restoring power to those who had been cut off. They worked in haste, for the storm had damaged a number of installations, and their services were urgently required elsewhere. Later they would return to do a more permanent job. It was not thought necessary, for the moment, to replace the red and white plastic strips.

The river dropped swiftly, as is the way of spate rivers. By nightfall the water was losing its burden of silt, and by morning it was running peat stained but clear. In the early afternoon the male osprey made a low pass over the bridge. His right wing struck the temporary power line, and he plummeted down into the water. He struggled to rise, but his wing was limp and useless. For a time he tried to oar himself across the water, but his feathers soon became waterlogged. The current swept him on down, and gradually he sank lower and lower in the water, until he disappeared beneath the surface.

Throughout that day the female called in vain for food, adding her voice to the incessant clamour of the chicks. By morning the male had still not returned. The female was in her sixteenth year, old and experienced, and twice before she had lost a mate. Now she knew the same fate had befallen her again.

There were fish in the loch below the eyrie, small and

14

undernourished though they were. Reluctantly she left the nest, and skimmed low over the loch. She took a fish at her first pass, and though it weighed no more than two ounces, it silenced the clamour of her young for the time being. So began a reign of terror for the trout in the loch. At first the fishing was easy, for the little trout had grown accustomed to the passage of the ospreys, but the survivors quickly learned to dive at the hint of a shadow, at the mere flicker of a wing. Instead of satisfying her needs, the female grew weaker and hungrier, for the effort entailed was greater than the reward.

High on the hill, Iasgair heard the clamour at the nest site. He had noted the absence of the male, and now, as he passed overhead bearing a trout to his favourite feeding place on the crag, he swooped down over the eyrie to take a closer look. At his approach the hen bird flew towards him, and at once, jettisoning his fish, he hastened to avoid her wrath. Instead of pursuing him, though, the female caught the falling fish neatly in her talons and flew with it straight to the nest.

As soon as he realised he was not being chased, Iasgair turned and made a low pass over the eyrie. The hen bird, engrossed in tearing slivers of flesh from the trout and feeding it to her chicks, barely glanced up at his passing, and he came to rest in the dead pine nearby. After about an hour he flew off, only to return with another fish. He did not surrender it at once, but perched in the tree, holding the trout in his talons and occasionally tearing at the head with his beak. Only when he heard the female give the hunger cry did he flap over to the eyrie, drop the trout on the rim of the nest, and fly away.

So he became foster parent to the widow and her fatherless family. In the weeks that followed he brought food regularly to the nest, until the young were fully fledged and making their first faltering attempts at flight. He made no attempt to forge any sort of bond with the female, and she was content merely to accept his offerings of fish. Only when the young were making their first clumsy flights from the eyrie to nearby trees did she spend any time away from the nest, and only rarely did she bring back food on her own.

The nights lengthened, and shooting stars blazed their brief trails of glory over the heavens. The heather spread its mantle of purple across the shoulders of the hills, and with the first frosts the leaves of the birch trees turned to coins of gold. Within a few days the young ospreys had taught themselves to fish, unaided, it seemed, for Iasgair made no attempt to teach them. Now they returned less frequently to the eyrie itself, perching instead in nearby trees, their plumage a little ragged and tatterdemalion, their movements often ungainly and awry. On occasion, when their hunting did not go according to plan, they still demanded to be fed, so that Iasgair grew weary of their importuning, but as each day passed they grew more proficient.

Of late Iasgair had begun to grow more and more restless. There was a sense of urgency in the air, as each morning the ground lay white with frost, and the cries of the wild geese passing south filled the sky. Soon the first snows would fall, and winter would claim the Highlands for its own. On a day in late September, when a stiff breeze drove fluffy white clouds from the north and set every tree in the forest creaking and swaying, Iasgair climbed high into the sky. Three times he flew in great sweeping circles over the valley that had been his summer home, as if imprinting its memory on his mind. Then, when he reached the southernmost point of the circle, he broke away and headed south into the sun.

For three hours he flew steadily south and west, at an altitude so high that he was barely visible from the ground except as a speck in the sky. Beneath him the ground undulated and rolled, fold after fold of mountain and hill, like the wrinkled, mossy hide of some primaeval beast, to which outcrops of rock clung like grey warty excrescences, and the occasional road lay like a wound stripe. Rivers flowed silver to the sea, and here and there a loch lay like a tear drop sparkling in the sun.

He was growing weary, for he had flown over sixty miles, and he was unaccustomed to such prolonged exertion. The feeling of restlessness had abated, and now hunger gnawed in its place. He had only a few hours' daylight left in which to find himself a meal, and a safe roosting place for the night.

A long narrow loch lay below, with a white ribbon of water at its mouth where a river flowed west to the sea. Sea trout were running with the tide, making their way through the loch and seeking the tributary streams that fed the loch, there to spawn in the clean gravel washed down from the hills. These fish were cousins to the brown trout that lived out their lives in the rivers and streams, but had chosen instead to emulate the lifestyle of their larger relatives, the salmon.

Spawned in the head waters, the infant fish spent the first two years of their lives in fresh water. Then, in the spring, they assumed mantles of silver, and migrated downstream and out to sea. Here in the rich feeding grounds of the salt waters they grew at a prodigious rate, returning each summer to the rivers of their birth. Some of the older survivors weighed as much or more than the salmon who journeyed alongside them, but the great bulk of the shoals was made up of smaller, younger fish. Many were immature, fish ranging from eight ounces to a pound in weight, not yet ready to spawn, but obeying the same instincts as their elders.

One of these died in the next instant, as Iasgair plucked it from the surface of the loch. Despite its small size, such was its strength that Iasgair was pulled briefly beneath the surface, until, flapping heavily, he rose in a shower of spray and bore his silver prize to a rocky island in the middle of the loch. Here he tore greedily at the firm pink flesh until he was satiated. Then he flew into the branches of a wind-twisted hawthorn, the only tree on the island, and as a red sun sank below the layer of cloud that rimmed the horizon, he fell asleep.

By morning the old restlessness had returned and he flew on. Beneath him the landscape began to change, a chequer-board of small fields and copses, of houses scattered among the trees, intersected by twisting roads along which cars and lorries scurried like ants. Ahead of him a grey-brown murk, a stain of carbon monoxide and pollutant smoke hanging in a cloud across the southern horizon, betrayed the presence of the industrial heart of Scotland.

Iasgair climbed higher, for even above the smoke pall the noxious fumes of sulphur dioxide and nitrous oxide fouled the air. When rain fell these pollutants would be washed from the sky, often miles away from their source, and the acids thus formed would fall on rock and tree and fern, eventually finding their way into lake and river and marsh and killing all life there. Iasgair flew faster, and soon the miasma was behind him, and he was crossing the rolling hills of the Border Country. Soon these too gave way to flat lands, and the mouth of a river meandering its way to the sea.

He reached the Solway Firth just as the tide was turning, the sea rushing over the flat sands at the speed of a galloping horse. Flounder were feeding in just a few inches of water, their presence betrayed by little spurts and clouds of silt. They were easy prey to a hungry osprey, and made a welcome change of diet. He might well have lingered on the estuary, but he was awakened in the early dawn by the clamour of jackdaws, who had found his roosting place in an ash copse. Their persistent attempts to drive him out at last wore down his nerve, and he flew off, low over the sands, where a flock of seagulls joined the chorus of jackdaws.

To the south mountains beckoned, low on the horizon, and for the next few days he drifted down through the Lake District, a miniature replica of Scotland with its lakes and rivers, moor and mountain, woodland and pasture. He took a small pike from Bassenthwaite, and a brace of perch from Derwentwater. Then he crossed the hills to Buttermere, where he surprised two anglers having a last day's trout fishing before the season ended. That night, in the bar of the hotel, one of them described how a great hawk had swooped down and snatched a fish from the water only yards from their boat.

His remarks were overheard by a bird watcher staying in the hotel, and he made a telephone call to a friend in Manchester. The friend told several of his acquaintances before he went to bed, and before dawn a small flotilla of vehicles was speeding north up the motorway, the occupants armed with binoculars, cameras and notebooks. By the time they converged on Lake Buttermere, however, Iasgair was fishing in Morecambe Bay, over twenty miles to the south, and after waiting in vain for the rest of the day the bird watchers were left to console themselves in the bar of the hotel.

From here Iasgair crossed the great sweep of Morecambe Bay, and south over the sea, with the Isle of Man and Snaefell low on the western horizon, and the industrial heartland of Lancashire to the east. Three hours later he was passing over the coast of North Wales.

The bracken on the hills was fading to yellow and brown, the rivers and lakes shrunken under a clear blue sky. In the rivers the sea trout, locally known as sewin, were gathering in the pools, awaiting the autumn rain and a passage upstream to the tributaries high in the hills. Iasgair loitered on his way south, feeding as he went. Sewin formed an important part of his fare, for the brown trout which once thrived in the Welsh hill stream were now greatly reduced in numbers.

In the days when coal mining flourished in the valleys, there was a constant demand for pit props to shore up the workings, and vast areas of the hillsides were planted with conifers to meet the demand. The hillside bogs were ploughed and drained, so that the rain, when it fell, ran straight into the streams, causing flash floods which swept the gravel beds away. At the same time acid rain from the industries in the south of Wales poisoned the spawning beds, so the young trout could not thrive. Then the mines were run down, closed almost overnight, but the need for softwoods remained, trees for paper and board.

The sewin had suffered too, and now they returned in fewer numbers than in years gone by. More ominous for the future of their kind was the fact that many of the fish returning to spawn were thin, undernourished fish. The demand for fish meal to feed cattle, pigs and poultry had led to overfishing by man, in particular the netting of sand eels, which provided an important part of the young sea trouts' diet. Still they survived, in sufficient numbers to procreate their kind, with some to spare to feed a hungry osprey. Whether they could support many of his kind was a question still to be answered.

The storm came without warning as he left the coast of South Wales behind. He flew on unheeding, for by now he was well accustomed to the turbulence of the skies. Instead he climbed higher, trying to escape the stinging lash of the rain squalls and the turmoil of the waves below, but he was totally unprepared for the violence of the gale. It was in fact no more than the dying tail of a hurricane spawned far out in the Atlantic, but it still brought torrential rain, and winds of a speed of fifty miles an hour, gusting to seventy and seventy-five.

He was in no immediate danger, for he was fresh and strong, but the winds slowed him down, forcing him off course and blowing him further and further east. Instead of passing the tip of Cornwall, he crossed the north coast of Devon, and as the light began to fade he pitched down in an oak wood on the fringe of Exmoor. Here he passed a disturbed night, amid the roar of the wind and the creak and groan of the tormented trees. Towards dawn however the wind dropped, and by morning the gale had blown itself out. He woke to blue skies and a fresh breeze, and hunger.

The great glaciers of the last ice age had ended far north of Devon, so there were no natural lakes in the hollows of the hills. There were rivers, some like the Taw and the Torridge, flowing north to the Severn Sea, and others like the Exe, flowing south, but all were swollen and turbulent with the rains, making fishing impossible. There were reservoirs, man made, but these were few. Iasgair passed one, hidden by the hills as he prospected low over the land, so it was two hours, and another forty miles, before he located one on the eastern slopes of Dartmoor.

Yet even here he was unsuccessful. The waters of the reservoir were whipped to white wavelets by the breeze, and even in the sheltered bays the ripples reflected the glare of the sun. After a dozen attempts he abandoned the reservoir and flew on down the river valley. It foamed beneath him, tumbling off the edge of Dartmoor, past green fields dotted with sheep, through precipitous gorges shaggy with oaks and pines, through thick woodlands into a flatter, broader valley where fat cattle grazed, and thatched cottages nestled beside winding roads. So he came to the estuary. The tide was running, and here at last he was rewarded, as flatfish, small plaice and flounders roved over the mudflats newly covered by the sea.

He might have lingered there, but the estuary was a noisy, busy place. A two-lane highway crossed the mouth of the river, and houses lay clustered over the surrounding hills. A nearby town gave off a busy hum and glare; a sewage works stood at the water's edge. He could have continued south, over the sea, but he was weary with the effort of the past two days. Instead, as dusk fell he returned inland, to the marshy water meadows a mile or so inland. Here, for one curious reason, he immediately felt at home.

For centuries, farmers in the valley had invested in trees, particularly oak and elm. Elm was always in demand, for it was almost as hard as iron and just as durable, being slow to rot and decay. The great naval dockyard thirty miles to the west took all they could supply, for wooden men o' war, and for piling for the wharves and jetties. Then steel plate took the place of wooden hulls, and concrete replaced wooden piling, so the great elms were left to decorate the countryside. Then came a disease, carried by a beetle imported from Canada, and it spread like a plague through the elms of southern England, killing off all the elms.

Some had been cut for firewood, but the wood needed a long drying out period before it was fit to burn, and even then it burned slowly, with a sullen flame and little heat. So most were left where they stood, and now their skeletons, bereft of bark and small branches, littered the landscape, towering above all other trees apart from the oaks and an occasional ash. They made ideal perches, enough roosting places for a whole colony of ospreys.

So he passed a comfortable night, and as he slept, as the tide ebbed and a half moon journeyed slowly across the sky, so the level of the river, which had been running bank high through the meadows, began to drop. As it fell it left behind a litter of flotsam, a tangle of branches, twigs and fern, plastic bottles and bags, binder twine and frayed ends of rope, lumps of polystyrene foam and empty beer cans, a dead chicken, tatters of clothing and other rags. Amongst the clutter was a great tree stump, torn from the bed of the river where it had lain all summer. Attached to it trailed the remains of a nylon fishing net, its gossamer snares almost invisible to the eye. In drifting downstream it had claimed one last victim, a sea trout, held by the gills and still flapping as it lay on the stones.

It was the first thing Iasgair saw as he woke to a dew-drenched dawn, and planing down off his perch he swooped down and grabbed the prize. With one claw fast in the fish he attempted to rise, only to find the fish refused to come free. He folded his wings and stood on the other leg as he attempted to wrest his prize free, and next moment he too was stuck fast, as the nylon monofilament of the net twisted tightly round his ankle. He struggled uselessly for a while, and then, letting the fish go, he tried again. Soon he was hopelessly enmeshed, with the nylon binding his wings and neck, so that although food was only a few inches away, he was powerless to reach it.

Chapter Three

Autumn lay in ruined splendour across the land, like the remains of a wedding feast after the guests had gone. Bees murmured drowsily among the mauve blossoms of the Michaelmas daisies, and wasps quarrelled over the remains of the pears that lay, ripe and rotting, in the tussocky, dew-drenched grass. The wind was soft and warm with the breath of the south, and a thin, high haze tempered the heat of the afternoon sun.

Nicola sat in her favourite place, under the walnut tree beside the pond, a half-empty glass on the table beside her, a magazine unopened on her lap. She felt guilty, and she knew why. David would have been appalled at the neglected state of the garden. Instead of idling away the afternoon over a glass of wine, he would have been mowing the lawn, dead heading the roses, cutting back the dying chrysanthemums and blackened dahlia stems, sweeping up the golden walnut leaves that lay strewn about her feet, filling the air with their incense. He could not bear untidiness, could not rest so long as a task remained unfulfilled.

A wasp buzzed angrily nearby, startling her out of her reverie, but as soon as she realised she was not the object of attack she paused to watch. The wasp had caught a crane fly, the daddy long legs of her childhood, the larvae of which wreaked such havoc among her carrots and potatoes. The weight of the unwieldy insect had brought the wasp to the ground, and she leaned forward in her chair to watch the combatants struggling in the grass, wondering how the wasp was going to deal with its prey.

The sting had done its work, and now the crane fly lay inert. Busily, the wasp went to work, cutting off the wings and legs. Then it picked up the carcase and tried to rise, but the weight was still more than the wasp could manage. Without any ado, the wasp cut the crane fly in half, and droned off to its nest, where it would feed the meat to its carnivorous grubs.

Nicola waited on, wondering whether the wasp would remember, and return for the other half. Sure enough, a few minutes later it was back, and after questing around for the space of a few seconds, it located the rest of the body and bore it away. She made a mental note to be more charitable to wasps in the future. The fewer crane flies there were in the garden, the better her carrots would fare.

David was right, she thought. He'd often said that you saw more of what was happening in the rest of the living world by sitting still for half an hour than by walking many a country mile. If only he'd practised what he preached, but he seldom did. Which, she mused bitterly, was probably why, at the ripe old age of thirty-nine, he had collapsed at the foot of their bed at seven o'clock one morning last spring, and was dead before she could summon any help. Afterwards she had come out into the garden, to this very spot. In the early morning sun the garden was ablaze with the gold of daffodils, the butter yellow of the primroses, and the fresh pale green of spring, and she had wept tears of shock, and anger at the injustice of anyone dying on such a perfect day.

The grief came later, and with it a great wave of inertia, a sense of futility which she recognised, in a vague way, and embraced as a sort of luxury. She had periods of remorse that they had been childless, followed by relief that she did not have the burden of bringing up a family on her own. On a more practical level, she was also relieved that David, with typical prudence, had taken out a life assurance policy, which now ensured that she did not have to worry about how to support herself. So she had drifted through the long summer, tending the vegetables he had sown, but neglecting the flower garden on which he had lavished such care.

She had been an only child. After the funeral her father and mother had invited her to sell up the house and go back to live with them in Kent, but she would be even more alone there than in Devon, acting as unpaid housekeeper in a town house, while her parents pursued their respective careers. Her mother was an editor of a glossy fashion magazine, commuting daily to London and working all hours, whilst her father was an executive of a travel firm, and was frequently abroad. Sometimes Nicola wondered what they would do when they both retired and got to meet each other. If she went to live with them she would also have to fend off her mother's incessant attempts at matchmaking, and as yet she didn't feel equal to the struggle. At least here in Devon she had the countryside she loved, and a few friends who were wise enough to leave her alone.

Drugged by the wine and sun, she drifted into an uneasy slumber. She had gained weight over the past few months, and her tight blouse and jeans accentuated the curves of her once trim figure. Her hands and feet were small, her face elfin and pointed, framed by shoulder-length dark hair. Her mouth was too large, her eyes, when they were open, a tawny gold, like those of a cat. She was thirty-seven years old, an awkward age, as she had remarked herself once – too old to start over again, but too young to stay a widow all her life. This was after several gins, at a party organised by some old friends of David's. The other guests had murmured sympathetically, and one man had taken advantage of her remark by holding her in an embrace that was rather too long and too close, but she could tell they were embarrassed, and she could have kicked herself for her display of self-pity. She had left the party soon after. They had been David's friends, not hers, and she had little in common with any of them.

A wren scolded her from a branch of the walnut tree above her head and she woke with a start, gazing up at the sky. The heat of the afternoon had drawn the moisture from the earth, banking it in fluffy grey clouds, white-edged with light, that ringed the horizon and left a patch of blue directly overhead. A buzzard hung there, climbing in slow circles high into the sky. She half thought to fetch the binoculars from the house, but decided there wasn't time, and continued watching until it was no more than a speck in the sky. Then she blinked, and the bird was gone, lost in the thin haze.

Suddenly she was lonely. Much of the pain of bereavement lay in not being able to share such small pleasures with someone of like mind.

David had been a professor of botany at the local university, but his interests had extended far beyond the plant world. He had pioneered the trend towards conservation, both locally and nationally, and with his enthusiasm and expertise inspired others to embrace the cause. He had organised campaigns, sat on half a dozen committees, lectured, cajoled, condemned, and, inevitably, involved Nicola.

She had transcribed his almost indecipherable notes, typed his speeches, chauffered him through the night, kept his diary and answered countless telephone calls with a diplomacy and tact which masked her lack of true commitment to the cause. It was not that she did not care. She had a deep and abiding belief in the sanctity of life, and a heartfelt love of the beauty of the natural world. Yet it was, to her, a personal, private religion. Too often, for her, it seemed that what passed for concern in others masked a desire for self-aggrandisement, or was merely an act of penance paid as the price for increasing affluence.

Still, she kept her opinions to herself, and so passed almost unnoticed in the shadow of her more flamboyant, ebullient husband. When he died a wave of panic swept through the ranks of his followers, but after the first flurry of phone calls there seemed to be a tacit agreement that she was not to be disturbed in her grief. Gradually the ripples of enquiry died away and she was left in peace. If not content, she was at least relieved she need no longer be so heavily involved.

Some friends at least remained staunch. People like Paul and Mary in the farm on the hill. They were in fact Nicola's nearest neighbours, and she was godmother to their baby son. At least, she mused, they were genuine country people, not just members of the growing army of townsfolk who were moving into the country, and adopting and adapting it as their own.

With a slight start she remembered that she was invited there for supper that very night. She would have to hurry if she was to be there on time. The blue sky had vanished. The clouds were thickening, growing darker and more ominous, and a restless breeze stirred the walnut, bringing one or two golden leaves fluttering down into her lap. Nicola shivered and got to her feet. A hot bath and a change of clothes were both long overdue.

The wind had strengthened as she left the house to walk the short distance to the farm. Already the distant moors were veiled in cloud, and a stinging rain was slanting across the fields, but the lane was sheltered and overhung with trees, and most of the rain passed harmlessly over her head. Paul was waiting for her at the farm gate, a golfing umbrella over his head, and together they raced up the drive to the open door, where Mary was waiting with a large gin and tonic held out as a prize.

The evening was fun, and perhaps because Nicola felt relaxed, and free to cry over her gin if she felt like it, she felt no desire to do so. She told them about her small adventure with the wasp, and Paul nodded. 'I've seen them strip every caterpillar off a whole crop of cabbages,' he said. 'Cheaper than insecticide, though mind, you have to pay them with plums.'

Nicola couldn't resist adding the bit about David. Mary smiled sympathetically. 'Of course, it's not everyone's idea of fun. I remember the wife of that ornithologist, what's his name, confiding in me after several drinks. "I hate bird watching," she said. "It always interferes with a good walk." There I was thinking she shared her husband's passion, and all the time she was just being a dutiful wife.'

There was smoked salmon with the drinks, served with lemon and slices of brown bread. Regretfully Nicola declined a third helping. 'This dress is too tight as it is,' she complained. 'I really must diet, or exercise, or both.'

'It's fish for the main course as well, I'm afraid,' said Mary. 'That's the price one has to pay for having an angler for a husband.'

The fish was delicious, pink and firm fleshed, served with a mixed salad and garnish dressing. 'Sea trout?' queried Nicola. 'I thought the season was ended.'

'So it has,' said Paul. 'But this is not sea trout. It's rainbow.'

'I've seen it on offer,' said Nicola, 'but I've never eaten it before. Rainbow trout are not native to this country, are they?'

'No,' said Paul. 'They come from the west coast of America originally, but they grow so fast that they've been bred commercially in this country for years now. Fortunately, or unfortunately, according to how you look at it, they don't breed in the wild over here, except in a very few rivers, so they have to be bred artificially, and raised in tanks until they are old enough to be sold as stock fish.'

'So you've taken to visiting fishmongers?' queried Nicola. 'And I thought you caught it yourself.'

'So I did,' said Paul. 'Fair and square. There's this guy up the valley. He's dammed a stream and created a series of artificial lakes which he has stocked, some with rainbow trout and some with brown trout of assorted sizes, which means I can go on fishing after the season has closed on the river.'

'So, if I've got this straight, you catch a fish that has been artificially bred and artificially raised, and swims in an artificial lake!' said Nicola.

'You forgot one thing,' replied Paul.

'What's that?'

'I caught it on an artificial fly!'

Nicola laughed. 'I like it. I suppose one could argue that by providing fisheries of this sort you are saving the wild stocks – the salmon and sea trout and brown trout of our rivers – from exploitation by anglers.'

'I look at it another way,' said Paul. 'The more anglers turn to fish the lakes, the more room there is on the river for those who prefer it. So I'm getting the best of both worlds.'

'What's he like, this fishery owner?' asked Nicola.

'A heron,' said Paul.

'He's quite dishy actually,' said Mary. 'Tall, lean, a bit military. Walks with a slight limp. Darkish, a bit thin on top. Wears a moustache. A bachelor, we think, but we're not sure. Why? Are you interested?'

'Certainly not,' said Nicola, applying herself once more to her fish. Suddenly the room felt warm, and she was surprised to feel herself blushing.

As they sat by the fire with coffee and liqueurs they were suddenly aware of the wind moaning in the chimney, and the lash of rain against the window. 'Sounds as though it's going to be a wild night,' said Mary. 'Would you like to stay here until morning?'

Nicola shook her head. 'Thanks, but it's not far, and I'll be sheltered in the lane. The fresh air will do me good, and blow some of these brandy fumes from my head.'

'So have one more to keep away the cold,' said Paul, rising to fill her glass. 'Maybe it will have eased a bit by the time you leave.'

If anything the weather had grown worse. Dark clouds obscured the moon, the air was filled with flying debris, twigs and leaves and drenching rain. The swaying trees roared against the force of the gale, and the lane was haunted by strange shadows that seemed to writhe and move. Far from being sheltered, the lane seemed to act as a funnel for the wind, which had shifted, and it buffeted against her, tearing at her clothing and threatening to throw her off balance. Leaning into it, she forced herself onwards.

At one point the lane dipped steeply downhill and she took it almost at a run, wobbling slightly on her high heels. So she did not see the branch that lay in her path until she had tripped over it and fallen headlong. Sobbing and laughing in turn, cursing herself for her stupidity, she picked herself up and staggered on, aware of her torn stockings and a warm trickle of moisture that she knew was not rain flowing from her left knee.

She reached the house, stripped herself of her wet clothes and stepped into the shower, running it first hot and then icy cold. Then she applied a dressing to her grazed knee and fell thankfully into bed. Even then she could not sleep, but lay tossing and turning, kept awake by the roar of the wind and the stinging pain in her leg. Towards dawn the wind dropped, and she fell into an uneasy slumber.

She slept late, and when she woke she ached in every limb, so she passed a lazy day and went early to bed. The next morning she felt invigorated and fresh. The storm had left a trail of havoc through the garden, tomato vines torn from

29

their canes, the fruit lying in the mud, runner beans askew on their poles, her winter sprout crop laid flat, their roots loosened in the soil. She worked steadily through the morning and most of the afternoon until at last, weary of her chores, she poured herself a drink and spent half an hour soaking in a hot bath.

Afterwards she still felt restless, but reluctant to face the garden again, so she put on her boots and her old gardening jacket and set off down towards the river. The sun was westering, flooding the brooding shoulder of the moor with light and gilding the bank of clouds that massed on the far horizon. The breeze was fresh against her cheeks, and the air heady with the smells of autumn. She thought of mushrooms, and for a while searched assiduously among the meadow grass, but the few she found were overgrown, ravaged by slugs, or broken by the grazing cattle.

So she turned to the river and walked along the bank, marvelling at the way the flood had cut into the soft soil bordering the stream. In places the turf was undercut, treacherous and crumbling, so she was careful not to encroach too near. A kingfisher piped its way upstream, a flash of azure blue drawn arrow-straight against the dark water. Somewhere a late running fish rolled, the deep hollow splash unmistakable in the silence.

She came at last to a great bend in the river. Here the water had cut a deep pool below a high bank where sand martins nested in the spring, and laid a sloping shore of shingle along the inside of the curve. She crunched her way across the gravel, shaking her head at the amount of rubbish borne down by the flood and wishing there was some way of getting the driftwood back to the cottage for her fire. Ahead of her lay a large tree stump, its roots a tangle of lesser rubbish, twigs and leaves and grasses. As she glanced at it, for a moment she thought she saw part of it move. She looked again, harder, suddenly uneasy at fear of the unknown. Surely it was a trick of the light, a wayward breeze.

She moved closer, wary of what she might find, and then, just as she had convinced herself it had all been a flight of fancy, she saw the movement again, and was suddenly aware of a great yellow eye watching her from among the debris.

Then she saw the shape of a large bird, hopelessly entangled in the remains of a fishing net.

For what seemed an age she just stood there, wondering what to do. She looked round for help, but she was alone. Then she knelt down beside it. The eagle, or whatever it was, gave one convulsive struggle and then lay still. Its eye closed, and the head fell forward. Even she could see it was close to death, and her immediate thought was to try to save it.

Her old gardening jacket was a depositary for all manner of things, plant labels and bits of twine, gloves, and a sharp pruning knife. Taking out the knife, she began to cut the bird free. It was not so easy as it had at first seemed, for the fine nylon had cut into the bird's legs and neck, and in places it was buried in the plumage, so that she was afraid she might injure the bird further. As she worked she noticed that the bird had a red ring on its left leg, bearing the legend K2, probably put there when it was a fledgling in the nest.

Now it was almost free, and only one wing remained trapped. She worked slowly and carefully, anxious not to damage the long flight feathers. From time to time her patient struggled feebly and the great claws clenched and unclenched, but it made no attempt to strike at her with its beak, and eventually she cut the last few strands of mesh. Then she took off her coat, wrapped the bird in it, and set off for home.

Chapter Four

She felt she must cut a faintly ridiculous figure. A small, slightly overweight woman in green wellies and jeans, marching along the river bank with what looked for all the world like a dead eagle tucked under one arm. She glanced furtively around, hoping no one she knew would see her, but the landscape was deserted, and now that the sun had sunk behind the moor dusk was gathering fast. As she walked, she tried to form some coherent plan of action.

First, she had to identify the wretched bird. Then she had to find some means of resuscitating it. A large cardboard carton. There was one in the garage. She had bought a new vacuum cleaner a few weeks earlier, and she'd kept the packaging in case she had to return it to the manufacturers. A hot water bottle, and plenty of newspapers. That would do for a start. If the bird survived the night she'd have to think about more permanent accommodation. Not for one moment did it occur to her to hand over her find to other, perhaps more capable hands. Much later, she was to wonder why. For the moment her only thought was to save the bird's life.

She laid her bundle on the kitchen table, lined the cardboard carton with newspaper, and put the kettle on to boil. Then she took her *Guide To British Birds* from the bookshelf and began to leaf through it. Rapidly she eliminated the smaller hawks and falcons, hobby, merlin, sparrow hawk, kestrel, peregrine. Then the harriers, buzzards and the eagle, until at last she was convinced that the bird she had found was an osprey. Only that couldn't be, because ospreys had been extinct in England for over a century. Then vaguely she

32

remembered reading that ospreys were once again breeding in the Highlands of Scotland. She also remembered, at some function she had attended in the past, a man saying to her, 'We give the breeding birds full protection, but we can't prevent the young being shot at as they migrate south over Spain in the autumn.' This didn't look like a young bird, but she assumed adults migrated too. Meantime, ospreys ate fish. There were some fillets of fish in the deep freeze, but they were of Dover sole. Keeping an osprey was going to prove expensive, until she could find an alternative.

Reluctantly she laid the fillets out to thaw and gingerly unwrapped the bundle on the table. The osprey was awake, alert, its indomitable eye watching every move she made, yet it remained passive, inert, making no attempt to struggle, even when she lifted it up and laid it in the box. She wrapped the hot water bottle in a towel and laid it near the bird's back, and then she closed the lid of the box and poured herself a drink while she thought out her next move.

The plain fact of the matter was that she didn't relish putting her hands near that great slashing billhook of a beak. She sat until the ice cubes in her glass had melted, and then she put another large slosh of gin in her glass, took a good swig, and went to where the fillets lay thawing by the sink. With a knife, she cut several long strips of flesh, and opening the lid of the box, she dangled one in front of the osprey's head.

The bird blinked, but otherwise took no notice. Gently she stroked the tip of its beak, waggling the strip of fish in what she hoped was a seductive manner. Still there was no response. At last, in desperation, she took hold of the beak in her right hand and forced the bird's head back. The beak opened quite easily. She dropped the fish into the gaping hole thus revealed and let the beak go.

Suddenly the osprey seemed to wake up. It shook its head, gulped twice, and looked around. Expectantly, she thought. Hurriedly she picked up another strip of fish and repeated the performance. The third time she produced the fish the osprey snatched it from her grasp before she had time to force feed it, and in a few minutes the entire fillet had gone. Triumphant, she closed the lid of the box and went to scrub the smell of fish from her fingers, wishing she had thought to wear rubber gloves for the operation. Suddenly she realised she too was ravenous, and utterly exhausted. If the osprey was still alive in the morning she would worry about it then. Meantime, all she wanted was food, a bath and bed.

She woke early, with the half-remembered feeling that she had something important to do. Then she recalled her patient, and slipping on a housecoat, she hurried downstairs.

She was quite unprepared for the devastation that greeted her. During the night the osprey had managed to find its way out of the box. A fillet of Dover sole had been transmuted into what seemed like several gallons of whitewash, liberally sprayed over the floor, the fitted cabinets, and the door of the fridge. The perpetrator crouched in one corner, its wings outspread. For a moment she stood, overwhelmed, half in awe at the sheer size of the bird, half fearful that it would attack her. She was tempted to open the kitchen door, there and then, tiptoe quietly away, and let the brute find its own way out to freedom, but then the osprey sat upright, folding its wings.

One settled neatly into place, but the right one, the wing which had been bound so tightly by the net, drooped lazily by its side, and she realised then that there was a danger that the osprey could not fly. Quietly closing the door, she retired to think things over. She did not feel equal to wrestling with the bird, injured wing or not, but she wanted her breakfast, or at least a cup of tea. She picked up the phone. It was time to summon the cavalry.

Almost before she had finished dressing she heard the growl of Paul's Landrover pulling into the drive. He was waiting on the step as she opened the front door. 'I've brought my biggest landing net,' he announced. 'The one I use for salmon fishing. Will it be big enough, do you think?'

'Come and look,' said Nicola, leading the way through to the kitchen.

Paul opened the door a crack and peered through. 'Dear God!' he breathed. He closed the door again and leaned his back against it, as if he feared the osprey would burst through. 'I can get the net over it, I think, but then what? What do you want to do with it?'

Nicola shook her head. 'I don't know,' she admitted. 'I could take it to the zoo, I suppose, or the RSPCA. They would know what to do with it. I just thought, if we could get it back in the box for the moment, it would give me time to think.'

Paul thought for a moment. 'Have you got a rug, or an old quilt? Once I put the net over it, it is going to struggle, and I don't fancy one of those talons in my hand.'

'There's an old sleeping bag,' said Nicola. 'I'll go and fetch it.'

Cautiously they moved into the kitchen, Paul holding the net at arm's length, Nicola bringing up the rear with the sleeping bag. From its corner the osprey watched them approach, but made no attempt to evade them, and even when Paul laid the net over its head it did not struggle. Nicola dropped the sleeping bag over the net and Paul picked up the bundle. Moments later the osprey was back in the box, with a few cookery books weighting down the lid.

Nicola's first thought was for coffee, and as she waited for the kettle to boil she stood over it, lost in thought. 'There's the fruitcage,' she murmured.

'For Heaven's sake woman!' Paul exploded. 'You're not thinking of keeping it! That's no budgie you've got there, you know. It'll cost you a fortune in fish, and in any case it's against the law to keep a wild bird.'

'The raspberries and strawberries are finished for the season. They won't come to any harm for a few days. I'm sure that wing isn't broken. All it needs is rest.' Carefully she spooned coffee into the mugs, then added sugar and milk. 'It's not against the law to render first aid, as long as I intend to release it as soon as it recovers.'

'You've gone all broody,' accused Paul. 'Heaven protect us from the maternal instinct.' He took his coffee and subsided into a chair.

'I shall need some sort of a shelter,' Nicola went on, as if he hadn't spoken. 'A tea chest or something.'

'Why?' asked Paul. 'He's never had any shelter in his life.'

'He hasn't been hurt before, and in any case, he must have

35

been able to get out of the weather, into a hollow tree or under a branch, or something. I don't know. I'd just feel happier if he could get under cover. How do we know it's a he?'

'We don't,' Paul admitted. 'I suppose we could fasten a plastic sheet over one end of the fruitcage.'

'So you will help?' said Nicola happily.

Paul groaned. 'I know when I'm beat. But not now. Later on today. I've got a farm to run, and I'm all behind as it is.'

Together they carried the carton up into the fruitcage and turned it on its side, leaving the osprey to find its own way out. 'He'll need a perch on a block,' said Paul. 'The sort of thing falconers provide, and food, and water of course. I'll bring a tarpaulin from the farm. It'll be better than a plastic sheet.'

With that he departed, anxious to get on with his chores, and Nicola was left to herself. She filled a large plastic bowl with water and set it just inside the fruitcage. It occurred to her that if the osprey perched on the rim of the bowl his weight could easily tip it over, so she set a large stone in the middle. The construction of a perch was beyond her for the moment, so she drove into town, bought half a dozen mackerel, some whiting, and herring. Rainbow trout were on offer but she refused to go to that expense. She found a block of wood, a section of elm log which had defied her attempts to split it for the fire, and rolled that into the fruitcage. Then she laid a mackerel and a whiting on the block and left the bird to its own devices. Finally, with mop and bucket and a bottle of disinfectant, she began to tackle the mess in the kitchen.

Afterwards she walked quietly up the garden path to the fruitcage to see how her patient fared. The osprey had emerged from the carton and was hunched disconsolately in one corner of the cage. The whiting lay untouched on the log but the mackerel had gone, and all that remained was the head, amid a scattering of silver scales. Reassured, she returned to the house to enjoy a rather belated breakfast.

Paul returned that evening, bringing with him the tarpaulin as promised, and also a long ash pole, a hammer, and some nails. 'He'll need a perch,' he explained, 'but until his wing heals he won't be able to fly up to one. So we'll fix this just off the ground, and gradually raise it higher as his strength returns.'

They worked until it was nearly dark. Apart from showing some signs of panic when they hoisted the tarpaulin over one end of the fruitcage, the osprey remained in his corner, regarding them with great yellow eyes as they fixed the perch in position six inches above the ground. He remained where he was long after they had packed up their tools and departed, until pale stars began to glimmer in the eastern sky. An owl flew down to perch on top of the fruitcage, regarded the great hawk for a while, and then, satisfied it presented no threat or rivalry, flew off on soundless wings in search of more profitable hunting grounds. Only then did Iasgair stir from his corner, walk slowly over to the perch, and jump up on to it. Already his wing was settling more firmly into place.

From then on there was little to do except to change his drinking water and ensure he had a fresh supply of fish. Paul had fixed nails at six-inch intervals into the uprights of the fruitcage, and it was a simple matter to raise the perch each day, tying it securely in place with stout twine, until at the end of a week it was three feet off the ground. As the days passed the osprey grew to welcome Nicola's appearance with food, and soon he was taking it from her hand. She was not sure she ought to encourage such familiarity, but since he was waiting for her at the door there seemed little she could do to prevent it.

After the storm the weather remained fine and unseasonably warm, and Nicola became aware of another problem which seemed to be insurmountable, and which daily grew worse. She mentioned it, as she led Paul and Mary along the garden path. 'Ospreys,' she said, 'present a waste disposal problem of awesome dimensions, not to mention a terrible pong.'

Indeed the whole fruitcage looked as if it had been liberally sprayed with whitewash, and a ripe smell of rotting fish hung over the garden. A host of flies buzzed incessantly around the pen, and the fate of next year's strawberry crop looked bleak. Yet in the midst of the squalor the osprey sat on his perch, dozing in the sun, his plumage as unmarked and pristine as the day he had arrived. He seemed totally oblivious to his surroundings, only twitching his head from time to time when the flies became too irritating.

'I've tried to clean up a bit,' said Nicola, 'but it's hopeless. I ought to dig up all the strawberries and spread gravel, but it would take tons.'

'If I'd thought about it, I could have brought a couple of bales of straw,' said Paul. 'That would have protected the plants, and afterwards we could have raked it all out. Still. It's a bit late now.' He studied the bird for some time. 'I think you could let him go,' he said at last. 'That wing is firmly back in place, and he must use it to get up on to the perch. If you keep him too long the muscles will get weak from lack of use.'

'Suppose he can't fly,' protested Nicola. 'I'd feel awful if I took him back down to the river and then discovered he couldn't fend for himself.'

'There's no need,' answered Paul. 'Just open the cage door. If he can fly, he'll find his own way back. If not, he'll still be in the garden, and you can carry on feeding him. In fact, I think you should do that anyway. Take his feeding block out of the fruitcage and leave a fish on top of it. If he's hungry, he'll come back for it.'

Nicola hesitated. Then, taking a last long look at her patient, she unfastened the door of the fruitcage and wedged it open with a brick. 'Come on,' she said. 'Let's go and have a cup of coffee.'

As they waited for the coffee to perk, Nicola lit one of her occasional cigarettes. She had given up smoking when she married, because David didn't approve of the habit, but after his death she had started again. Even so, she felt a slight twinge of guilt every time she smoked one. 'I wonder where he'll go?' she pondered.

'I expect he'll move on south,' answered Paul. 'I've been reading up a bit of their history. Odd birds. They haven't changed their lifestyle for millions of years apparently. In fact they never do anything in a hurry. Each autumn they drift slowly down to West Africa, and in spring they fly back to Scotland. They don't breed until they are three or four or even five years old, but they live a long time. If no one shoots them, that is.'

'It would be an awful waste of our time and effort if someone shoots this one,' remarked Nicola.

'We'll never know,' said Mary. 'At least you saved him from death by starvation. The French and Spanish used to have a reputation for shooting everything that flies, but from what I've heard they have become a lot less trigger-happy these days. The conservation movement is no longer confined to these shores.'

Later that afternoon Nicola went to the fruitcage, fully expecting to find it empty. To her surprise the osprey had not moved, but remained dozing on his perch. Paul was right about ospreys never doing anything in a hurry, she thought. She wondered whether she ought to feed him again. There were still a few mackerel in the deep freeze, and it seemed a pity to waste them. On impulse she rolled the wooden block out of the cage on to the lawn, and then went back to the house to collect one of the fish.

It took a little while to thaw out. The osprey awoke from his reverie when she laid the fish on the block, and half spread his wings as if to fly down from his perch. Then, when Nicola made no move to take the fish to the cage, he lost interest. 'Stupid dumb bird!' exclaimed Nicola in exasperation. 'Why don't you take your freedom when it is offered?'

As if in answer the osprey folded his wings and turned his head away. For a moment Nicola was tempted to go inside the fruitcage and drive him out, but finally she shrugged and went off back to the house. Next morning the mackerel was gone, and so was the osprey.

Chapter Five

Dawn flooded the valley with golden light, the warmth of the sun driving the mist from the hollows and drawing tendrils of vapour from the freshly ploughed fields. Pheasants in all the glory of their autumn panoply scratched for acorns beneath the oaks, and maples flamed yellow in the hedge-rows. It was the little summer of Saint Luke, the time of the fat, when bird and beast alike feasted before the long drawn famine of winter.

Iasgair surveyed the scene from his roost high in the branches of the dead elm tree by the river. The pain in his wing had subsided during the night and he felt fresh, alert, and hungry. After he had left the fruitcage he had snatched the mackerel from the block and flown off with it high into the sky. Circling round, he had located the river winding across the valley floor, and the stark white branches of the tree on which he had spent his first night in the valley. So he had made his way there in the gathering dusk. A casual observer would have noted nothing amiss in his flight, but long before he reached the tree the strain on his wing had begun to cause him discomfort. He did not know it, but it would be some time before the injured wing was strong enough to carry him over any distance.

Not that he had any intention of going anywhere. Maybe it was the trauma of becoming ensnared, and his resulting incarceration, maybe it was the unseasonably warm weather, or maybe it was simply the security afforded by his perch in the dead elm. Perhaps it was a combination of all these factors which drove all thoughts of further migration from

40

his mind. Instead his one thought at the moment was food.

He lofted down from his perch, and circling, began to climb. A hundred feet above the river he began to follow its course. The water was once more low and clear after the long fine spell. Late running sea trout, small fish of between ten and fifteen inches in length, were lying quietly in the pools, together with an occasional salmon, waiting for the rains to swell the river and aid their passage upstream. Checking in his flight, he circled lower, and dived on the first shoal.

The river ran from west to east, and the morning sun was at his back. Even as he swooped, his shadow fell across the shoal, and immediately, without panic or fuss, the fish seemed to melt away, gliding into the deep fast water by the bank where he could not reach them. Undaunted he flew on, round a bend in the river, searching until he had located a second shoal. This time he came upon the fish unawares, but even so he failed to make a kill.

He was used to failure, particularly with such elusive fish as these, but as he drew blank a third time he became aware of a now familiar ache in the muscles of his left wing. As he climbed, dripping from the water, shaking himself to throw off the weight of excess moisture, he knew he would shortly have to rest. High in the sky, he found a thermal, a rising current of warm air, and rode it with wings outspread, resting on a blanket of air and swinging round in a great circle. So he passed over the garden he had left the night before, and his keen eyes espied a fish laid out on the block in the middle of the lawn.

Without hesitating, he dropped down and snatched up the fish, but rather than carry it back to the elm he took it up on top of the fruitcage. There he proceeded to tear strips of flesh from the bones, and he was just gulping down the last remains when Nicola emerged from the house. Startled by her appearance, Iasgair prepared for sudden flight, but then recognising her as harmless, he folded his wings and watched her as she made her way slowly towards him.

For a long time she stood, lost in admiration. She was aware of a deep sense of satisfaction and pride at her achievement. It was one thing to keep a bird in a cage. It was infinitely more gratifying to have one return of its own free

41

will. Her delight was mingled with a faint sense of unease that a creature born wild should place such trust in her, and so perhaps in others who might well abuse that faith. It occurred to her that she should chase the bird away, frighten it so much it would not return, but she could not escape the nagging thought that it may yet be dependent on her for some time, at least as a source of food. True freedom, she reminded herself, for human and animal alike, was freedom from hunger, freedom from hardship and pain, not simply freedom to come and go and wander the world at will. Thoughtfully she returned to the house, leaving Iasgair to digest his meal in peace.

Iasgair stayed perched on top of the fruitcage for most of the morning. He had quickly learned that the ache in his wing subsided as long as he did not fly, and once he was full fed he was content to sit and doze in the sun. His tranquillity was disturbed by a pair of marauding magpies, prospecting the garden for anything edible they could find. Their angry chatter attracted a crow, who flew down to see what the commotion was all about. For some time the trio contented themselves with scolding Iasgair from the branches of a nearby ash, but after a while one of the magpies grew sufficiently emboldened to fly over his head, close enough to make him duck. Then the other birds joined in, circling close and kicking out at him as they swooped past. At last Iasgair could endure their torment no longer, and flew off back to his perch in the elm. The magpies followed as far as the edge of their territory before abandoning the chase, and the crow, finding himself alone, gave up soon after.

The dead elm which Iasgair had chosen as his roost was ideally situated. It stood in one corner of the meadow bordering the river, well away from the footpath that followed the course of the stream, but commanding a clear view of the fields around. Most of the land was permanent pasture, waterlogged in winter, luxuriant with flowering grasses and plants in summer, tenanted by browsing herds of cattle.

Iasgair passed the next few days resting in the elm, huddled immobile against the trunk. Although he was plainly visible at all times no one noticed him there. Few people ever bothered to look up, and if they did, it was only to take in the scenery with a passing glance.

Each morning at first light he flew over to the garden, where a fish was laid ready for him on the block. With each flight his wing grew stronger, and the pain was now no more than a slight ache. On the second morning he surprised Nicola making her way along the path to the lawn, and swooped down low to meet her. For a moment she almost dropped the fish and ran, but a mingled sense of fascination and awe held her transfixed as she watched the majestic beat of his wings, so slow and yet so powerful, carrying him towards her almost at eye level. At the last moment he stalled in his flight and soared over her head, climbing high into the sky and then circling round as she placed the fish on the block and stepped back. Then he dropped like a stone, snatched the fish from the block with one outstretched talon, and climbed high into the sky before heading rapidly back to the river. Nicola walked slowly back to the house, trying to calm the rapid beating of her heart. Iasgair took the fish back to the elm, and afterwards, full fed, closed his eyes against the morning sun.

The river bank was a favourite playground for people from the nearby town. In summer they came to picnic, and to bathe in the stream, despite the risk of sickness from the treated sewage effluent that was discharged up river. Throughout the year the footpath was used daily by people of all ages. Whole families came to walk, to cycle, to jog, and to exercise their dogs. Many people were no longer content with owning just one dog but now kept two or more, and with the increase in crime owners favoured large, aggressive breeds – alsatians, dobermans, rottweilers, bull terriers – to guard their property and their lives.

For the most part the humans kept to the river banks and the winding path that led across the meadows. The dogs were a different matter. They were allowed to wander free, the whole object of the exercise being to encourage them to rid themselves of the surplus energy they had acquired cooped up in houses for most of the day. So they ran riot over the fields and along the river banks, flushing ducks and wading birds out of the reeds, scattering shoals of fry in the sun-warmed shallows, chasing field voles through the short tussocky grass of the meadows, sending shock waves to shatter the calm of countless small lives. Meanwhile, oblivious to everything except the welfare of their pets, the owners looked on in smiling approval.

On the afternoon of the third day a young woman parked her hatchback on the road near the bridge. Three little dogs spilled out on to the road, milling around in excitement and barking hysterically. Their tails, if they had any, would have been wagging, but they were corgis, bred for over a thousand years to work as cattle dogs in Wales, but now relegated to the role of court jester in countless suburban homes throughout the land.

The dogs had squeezed under the gate and into the field almost before the woman had locked the car. Unconcerned, she let them go. She knew they wouldn't bother any livestock grazing in the meadows, and there was no harm they could come to. She followed them through the gate and wandered along behind them. By the time she had crossed the first meadow they were a hundred yards ahead of her.

Had they run in a straight line they could have trebled the distance. Instead they ran to and fro, quartering the meadow, their short legs covering the ground with amazing speed. With each step they grew nearer and nearer to a young buck rabbit, crouched in a clump of bracken fern close to the hedge.

A few yards would have led him to safety among the tangle of roots and thorns that protected the hedge bank. Unfortunately, one of the corgis came up between him and the hedge, cutting off his retreat. At once he bolted for the corner of the meadow, and the dead elm that stood there. The trunk of the elm was hollow at the base, and there was a hole he could just squeeze through.

He made it with inches to spare, the white teeth of the nearest dog snapping at his heels, and crouched there in the musty darkness, waiting for the hammering of his heart to subside. Outside the corgis raced around the base of the tree, yapping their excitement and scrabbling at the trunk. High in the tree Iasgair reacted to what he assumed was a direct assault on his citadel, and dropped off his perch.

The first the corgis knew of it was the whistle of his pinions as he swooped to attack, a great black shadow coming out of the sun. They fled in panic as his talons slashed out, narrowly missing catching one of them across the rump. Across the meadow the woman stood in stunned disbelief, and then she screamed as the dogs raced back towards her, Iasgair in pursuit. For a moment she was tempted to stand her ground in defence of her pets, but after one look at the bird's wing span her nerve failed her and she fled, stumbling across the meadow towards the safety of her car. Halfway there the corgis passed her, but Iasgair had long ago given up the chase. Circling high in the air, he flew back to the elm.

Half an hour later the woman was still shaking, and after she had fortified herself with a large glass of dry sherry she telephoned her husband at his office to tell him about her ordeal. 'Are you sure it wasn't a buzzard?' he asked.

'Of course I'm sure. I see buzzards every day when I'm walking the dogs, and this one was much too big. In any case buzzards have never attacked like this one did. I thought it was going to carry little Taffy away. Something ought to be done. It's dangerous. At least you could warn the farmer.'

The husband was a salesman for a firm of agricultural merchants and he knew all the farmers in the area, at least by name. Privately he thought he was wasting his time, but he knew better than to argue. 'I'll give him a ring,' he promised, 'but I doubt if there's much he can do.'

After his wife had rung off he dialled the number of Holly Brook Farm, expecting the farmer to be at work in the fields at that hour of the day. As it happened Paul was in the farm kitchen, snatching a hasty mug of tea before he started the milking. He listened politely to what the caller had to say, thankful the other man couldn't see his face. 'I do sympathise,' he replied, 'and I hope your wife hasn't suffered too much from her ordeal, but I really don't see what I can do. If there is an eagle on my land, it's a protected bird under the law. In any case, I must remind you that the right of way is restricted to the footpath. Any person who leaves it, or allows their animals to stray, is technically trespassing.'

To Paul's relief, the caller was disinclined to argue. 'I merely wanted to warn you about its presence, in case it poses a threat to your livestock, or attacks any other walkers or their dogs. They might make a fuss.'

'I've got no lambs in the water meadows,' said Paul. 'The ground's too wet for them at this time of year. As for the public . . . They'll just have to take their chance. Meantime, I don't think it would be a good idea to broadcast the news. It might have the effect of attracting the public, rather than keeping them away.'

As he put the phone down he glanced across at Mary, who was grinning like a school girl. 'Nicola's baby?' she queried.

Paul nodded. 'Sounds as though he's recovered his health and strength. Let's hope he pushes off to Africa or wherever he's going before he attracts too much attention.'

Mary reached for the phone. 'All the same, perhaps I ought to warn Nicola not to let on why she has suddenly grown so fond of fish.'

Yet even as she spoke, Paul's fears were being justified. After she had spoken to her husband, the woman had called several of her friends who also walked their dogs by the river to warn them of the risk. They in turn called others, and soon, like a bush fire out of control, the news spread. Shortly after first light the road by the bridge was jammed with traffic, and the path by the river was lined with spectators, many with cameras and binoculars. There was a reporter there from the local newspaper, accompanied by a press photographer, and close behind was a crew from regional television. Before long someone lifted the field gate off its hinges, and a fortune in the latest Japanese technology, shiny and metallic as beetles, streamed across the meadow in four wheel-drive. Standing beside a police patrol car, its flashing blue light adding to the lustre, a bewildered constable talked urgently into his handset. Nicola, who had walked down to the river in the hope of seeing her osprey, took one look at the gathering and fled.

The excitement died as swiftly as it had flared. As hour after hour passed without a sighting of the strange bird

46

people began to drift away. By early afternoon the meadow was deserted except for a morose little group in anoraks and green wellingtons. Tripods with their cameras and telescopes remained unmanned as their owners stood about with their hands in their pockets, talking about other sightings, other journeys in search of rare birds. Some had driven down from Bristol and the Midlands, and now they were cold, tired and hungry, and the last of the coffee in their flasks had gone cold. Yet they were reluctant to give up, even though the elm stood empty and deserted in the corner of the meadow. As they waited a latecomer arrived, a birdwatcher who had driven down from Coventry. He realised, even before he got within hailing distance of the group, that his journey had been a waste of time.

The fish Nicola had left on the block that morning lay untouched. Perhaps the osprey had been captured, or shot? Mingled with this fear, she was suddenly aware of a deep sense of guilt as she realised that for the past week she had been so involved with the osprey that she had scarcely spared a thought for David. It occurred to her then that all the old clichés were true, that work was a panacea for grief, that caring for others was the best cure for self-pity. Perhaps, if she cared enough . . . But she dismissed the idea as soon as it arose. To take up some charitable cause, merely to forget, would be unfaithful to David's memory, and anyway, it wouldn't work.

Meantime she fretted about the welfare of the osprey, and her friendship with Paul and Mary. Would they blame her for the circus taking place down by the river, and the state of the meadow, trampled and churned into mud? She was vastly relieved when Paul rang her that evening with an amusing account of the events of the day, and to tell her that the object of all the interest had disappeared. 'He may be back,' he said, 'but my guess is that he has left us for the winter. Thanks to you, he's been granted a new lease of life.'

With that, for the moment, she was content.

Chapter Six

After the dogs had gone Iasgair returned to his perch in the elm, but he could not settle. His sanctuary had been violated, and he came awake at every small sound – the flutter of a bird's wing, the call of a crow, the sharp, dry cough of a bullock in the neighbouring field. Twice he lofted from his perch, circling round the meadow before he returned. The sun was westering, and soon darkness would fall. As if coming to a decision he took off once more, this time flying up the valley, following the course of the river.

Beyond the flat meadowland the valley narrowed, the fields giving way to low steep-sided hills, their flanks strewn with great boulders of granite. Here dense oak woods grew, mixed with a scattering of beech, ash and chestnut. The woods looked primaeval, the oaks ageless and immortal, but this was an illusion. Most of the oaks had been planted a century before, and their tops had been pollarded every ten years or so to supply bark for the tanning industry, and the stripped branches turned into charcoal. But gradually coal replaced charcoal for fuel, and imports of cheap leather killed the local tanning industry, so the woods fell into disuse.

The oaks grew unchecked, twisted and awry, shutting out the light in summer, but allowing a thick growth of wild flowers and bracken in the spring. Badgers and foxes moved in to make their lairs in the hollows under the rocks, rabbit and vole and hunting stoat sheltered under the canopy, and sparrow hawks nested in the trees. Gradually the wilderness reclaimed the woodlands for their own, and only the shy roe deer followed the twisty footpaths beneath the trees.

In a clearing stood a solitary old ash, towering above the oaks that had hedged it around. Its crown had been blasted by lightning in a summer storm a decade ago, and now the dead limbs shone silver in the fading light. The tree was already hollow when the lightning bolt struck, and the trunk, filled with twigs and leaves and the debris of generations of birds' nests, burst into flame. The fire spread, blighting the forest around, but then came the rain, extinguishing the flames before they could extend too far. Miraculously, it seemed, the tree still clung to life, each spring sending forth a few feeble shoots of tender green. Here, as the sun set beyond the brooding shoulder of the moor, Iasgair came to rest.

He woke to grey dawn. Slowly, the tips of the oaks were suffused with golden light as the sun rose over the sea. A clamour of rooks filled the air, and somewhere further down the valley a tractor coughed into life. Far below the river foamed and chattered over its rocky bed, as if impatient to reach the peace and tranquillity of the fat, fertile meadow lands further down the valley.

For a long while Iasgair remained motionless, crouched on his perch and basking in the thin warmth of the early morning sun, until at last hunger drove him into the skies. The oaks grew sheer down to the water's edge, overhanging the stream until their branches touched on either side. Here and there glimpses of the river revealed deep pools and guts where the white water foamed into pots and chasms between the rocks. There were long stretches of fast, shallow, sunlit water where tiny trout hovered in mid-stream waiting for morsels of food swept down by the current. Only one stretch, canal-like and alder lined, where the river's haste was impeded by the low wall of a weir, offered the chance of a fish.

A hundred feet above the stream Iasgair floated on lazy wings, hovering from time to time, his head turning from side to side as he inspected the surface of the water. There were trout, sea trout, just below the surface, but most lay prudently in the shelter of the alder trees. One fish, a big one, lay further out in the stream, about a foot below the surface. Iasgair drifted over it, turned, dropped fifty feet and came in on a long, slanting dive. He hit the water in a shower of spray, and in an instant one talon gripped the fish firmly across the back.

Next moment Iasgair was pulled under as the fish surged away. Grimly, wings rowing the water, his claws sinking further into living flesh, Iasgair struggled to rise, but the fish was too powerful for him, and once again his wing proved unequal to the strain. When he was dragged under for the second time and the fish showed no sign of weakening, Iasgair reluctantly relaxed his grip. The fish wobbled away into the depths, and shaking himself like a dog to rid himself of excess moisture Iasgair flew heavily back to his perch on the ash. He sat for a long time, wings outspread to dry, and then began the long, laborious routine of rearranging his plumage. The sea trout was mortally wounded, and after a while it floated to the surface and began to drift towards the weir, speeding up as it neared the sill. Then the current caught it and swept it away downstream to oblivion and the waiting sea.

His plumage restored to his satisfaction, and his wing thoroughly rested, Iasgair flew down to the river again. The sea trout had all faded from sight, in that mysterious way they have, but brown trout were feeding on the flies that danced over the surface in the warmth of the sun. Iasgair plucked a fish of about half a pound out of the water on his first pass, and returned in triumph to the ash tree.

For the next three days Iasgair fished the long pool above the weir. The sea trout remained elusive, sheltering under the overhanging alders, or fading from sight on his approach, but with the brown trout he was more successful, managing to take a fish each day. Then the long fine spell came to an abrupt end as a depression raced in from the Atlantic, bringing rain-laden clouds driven by a gale force wind. The burden of moisture was almost too much for the clouds to bear, and most of it spilled on to the high moors, saturating the peat bogs, filling the tributary streams and swelling the volume of water in the river, so that by morning what had been a crystal clear current was now a turbulent brown flood. The salmon and sea trout, which had been waiting for such an event, surged forward against the current, rejoicing in the spate, running the weirs, leaping out of the water in their haste to reach the spawning grounds high up on the moor.

Iasgair passed a wakeful night, as all round him the oaks roared in defiance of the wind, and the old ash tree creaked and groaned beneath him. Despite the gale the tree held firm, for even in death the timbers were resilient and strong. The osprey's thick, oily plumage shed the rain, and the air trapped in the under feathers insulated him against the cold, so he felt no discomfort. Towards dawn the wind abated, and he slept long into the next day, as the rain fell and the river continued to rise. Under these conditions fishing was impossible. The only thing to do was to conserve energy, and wait.

The second day dawned clear, with a brisk breeze polishing the sky with white cotton wool clouds. Iasgair left the ash and climbed high into the sky, questing in ever widening circles above the river. To the east lay the estuary. The tide was out, and the glistening mud flats were thronged with birds, redshank and plover, oystercatcher and curlew, shelduck, sandpiper and knot. A heron stood motionless among the reeds, Canada geese grazed on the sparse grasses, and here and there splashes of white marked the presence of swans.

To the south was the glimmering expanse of the sea, girded by steep cliffs, iron grey in the sun, and to the west and north the dark, brooding shoulder of the moor. All around the rolling oak-clad hills of Devon lay like a rumpled blanket over the earth. Iasgair flew upstream, following the twists and curves of the river as it wound its way through the landscape.

Some distance upstream a tributary entered the river. Nowhere was it more than a foot deep, nor more than a yard wide, and it was but a few short miles to its source, but it possessed a quality the main river lacked. Its waters were alkaline, and rich in the calcium salts which were the building blocks of life.

When the great granite mass which is now Dartmoor thrust skywards some two hundred and fifty million years ago, it broke through a crust of older, metamorphic rock which earlier still had been the bed of a tropic sea. This older rock, this limestone, formed from the bodies of countless small sea creatures over the ages, was pushed aside by the granite. Most of it had eroded away, but there was left a remnant, a metamorphic ring, that surrounded the moor and still surrendered its ancient wealth to the land. This particular stream had its source at the foot of a low limestone cliff through which the rainfall had percolated down through the centuries. Its waters were rich, and they were pure, being free from the pollutants that had come more and more to contaminate the land. By contrast the water from the moor was often acid in nature, so much so that at times it dissolved out the aluminium present in the granite, inhibiting insect life, and sickening the fish.

Throughout the centuries the stream flowed across the land, while generations of farmers watered their livestock from its banks, and harvested the rich hay crops that grew in the few meadows along its length. Their wives used the water to brew their home-made wines, and watched their children grow up sturdy and strong of bone. Fishermen knew that where the tributary joined the main stream the trout were bigger and fatter than elsewhere.

Then the old widower who had worked the land for the past seventy years died, and the son who inherited it had no use for the rambling, tumbledown old farmhouse and the few acres of pasture that remained with it. So he left its fate in the hands of an estate agent and returned to the coast. His caravan park on the cliffs yielded a better harvest than the heaviest crops of hay. He thought he might have to wait a long time before the old place was sold, but to his surprise the estate agent found a buyer almost straight away, without him having to lower his price.

The new owner knew little of geology or biology, but he had taken advice before making his purchase. Martin Collier had been an officer in the marines. He was tall, with lank dark hair and a slim moustache he was always meaning to shave off, and a thin physique which belied his physical strength. 'All wire and whipcord,' was how his platoon sergeant described him. He had led his platoon into action on a remote island on the other side of the world, until a stray sniper's bullet had shattered his left thigh bone. The surgeons had saved his leg, but it was left an inch shorter than the other, and still pained him from time to time.

Though at times he raged against the pain and the frustration of his incapacity, he bore no animosity towards the unknown Argentine who had so summarily cut short his military career. He was a man, doing a job the same as himself. Faced with the alternative of a desk job or early retirement, he had chosen the latter, and come to live in the Devon countryside he knew and loved so well.

He had taken advice, and won the blessing of the planning authority. Then he brought in expert help – surveyors, landscape architects, bulldozer drivers, biologists from the River Authority. A firm of local builders set about restoring the dilapidated old farm house, and two labourers, an old man and a boy, attacked the neglected and overgrown gardens.

The next three months proved to be a time which, in retrospect, he would rather forget. Nothing in his army career had prepared him for the logistics of coordinating the work of a small army of men, all of whom seemed to have their own idea of what to do, and who seemed bent on spending twice as much money as he possessed. There were days of frustration and delay, evenings spent battling with a mountain of paperwork, juggling accounts, nights when he lay awake, despairing of ever realising his dream, but at last there came an evening in early spring when he stood alone, looking out of his bedroom window at the transformation of his small domain.

Where once a tiny water course flowed through overgrown meadows there were now three irregularly shaped lakes, strung like jewels along the length of the stream, all rapidly filling with water. As yet they were devoid of life, and the land around was naked, raw, but already he could visualise the scene planted with trees and shrubs, grasses, wild flowers and ferns. Already the lakes were beautiful, pearly white in the dawn, ruby red darkening to deepest garnet in the setting sun. He tried to picture them in the years to come, reed fringed and lily strewn, the haunt of newts and frogs, of water birds and dragonflies, and, of course, fish. He could foresee a lifetime of work ahead, of sowing and planting and without doubt of continually pruning back the more exuberant growth. Meantime he had a clean slate on which to draw, with the forces of nature to guide his hand.

All that had been two years ago, and now he was just beginning to enjoy the fruits of his labours. He had stocked the lakes with trout – native brown trout, and exotic rainbows from the west coast of America. He bought the trout from a hatchery, the bulk of them fish between a pound and two pounds in weight, plus a number of heavier fish between three and six pounds apiece. Occasionally, when he could afford them, he added a few leviathans in excess of ten pounds.

Once the first batch of fish had settled in, he had taken his old split cane rod and a slow-sinking fly line and gone down to the lakes to fish. It was a warm evening in May. The sun was setting, and the surface of the lake rippled like shot silk in the soft southerly breeze. He attached a tapered nylon leader to his line and tied a small green nymph to the tip. He cast out into the lake, counted slowly to five to let the nymph sink, and began slowly to retrieve his line.

For the first two casts nothing happened. On the third he waited longer, counting to ten before he began his retrieve, and within seconds he felt a sudden savage pull. His reel screamed and the rod bucked in his hand as the fish tore off line in its first wild run across the lake. He saw the gleam of a gold flank as it turned, and then it was zigzagging back towards him, forcing him to back away as he stripped in the excess line. Then it dived, and swam in slow circles, jerking the rod savagely as it shook its head. Gradually it weakened, there was a feeble flopping on the surface, and then it turned on its side and slid towards him. Bending down, he freed the hook from its jaw without taking the fish from the water, and watched it slide away back into the depths.

That was the first and last fish he ever caught in his lakes. That there was a certain skill involved, in choosing the right lure and in presenting it correctly, could not be denied, and a cool head was needed in playing the fish. But the fish were there to be caught, and once hooked they had nowhere to go but the confines of the lake. He still fished regularly, but in the river for salmon and sea trout and the little wild brown trout that haunted every run and eddy. He left the fish in his lakes for others, and he provided such good service and value for money that the little valley had become a Mecca for anglers from all over the country. He charged high prices, but he regulated the number of anglers permitted to fish in any one day, and there was always a waiting list of fishermen eager to try their luck.

He was not rich, but he enjoyed living frugally. His lifestyle left little time for socialising, but he preferred solitude. He had never married, because he felt that the armed services and marriage were two conflicting states perpetually at war, and his observation of his fellow officers and men tended to reinforce this view. Yet he was content. He had his music, his books, and the ever changing panorama of life in his secluded valley for comfort.

Indeed his bedroom, with its wide picture window overlooking the lakes, had proved an ideal observation platform for watching the wild life which had so readily adopted this newly formed territory. The lakes were named after birds he had first sighted on them, Heron, Kingfisher, and Grebe. He kept a pair of binoculars handy on the windowsill, and spent many hours just sitting and watching, justifying the time stolen from more pressing affairs by telling himself that it was as effective as making a foot patrol around the lakes.

So, on this fine late autumn morning, dressed and shaved and ready for his breakfast, he lingered on at the window. The little valley was sheltered from the wind that drove the clouds across the sky, so only the faintest ripple disturbed the surface of the lakes. A moorhen scouted busily along the fringe of reeds, and the pair of Canada geese that had adopted him that autumn grazed on the grassy verge of the nearest lake. He tolerated them, because although their copious droppings were a mess, they made efficient lawn mowers. Then, one of the geese cackled a warning, and a great bird flew upstream from the direction of the main river, circling the furthermost lake, the one called Heron. As he watched it swooped down in a long, slanting dive and snatched a rainbow trout from the water.

Almost before he could reach the binoculars resting near

his hand the bird was climbing high into the sky. Then he just had time for a close up view before the bird disappeared in the direction from which it had come. He felt a great wave of excitement break over him, a feeling of exultation, of almost savage joy. He had recognised the bird at once, but he had never seen one in the flesh before, and never in his wildest dreams had he expected to see one in his valley. He guessed it must be a migrant on its way south.

Regretfully he laid down the binoculars and went downstairs, telling himself he was privileged to have had an experience which occurred perhaps once in a lifetime. Only later, as he was eating his boiled egg, did he reflect rather ruefully that his momentary glimpse of the osprey had cost him the price of a fish.

Chapter Seven

A week later Martin Collier turned his back on his small kingdom and headed up the valley, driving his car along the narrow twisting lanes that followed the course of the river up on to the moor. He felt on edge, irritated, and he knew why. Instead of continuing its journey south, the osprey had come each morning and deprived him of yet another fish. Each one had cost him over a pound to buy from the hatchery, and it was money he could ill afford to lose. After the third day he had seriously thought of getting his shotgun out of the steel cabinet in his study and blowing the osprey out of the sky, but in his heart he knew he could not do it. Quite apart from the fact that it was illegal to shoot a protected bird, he had too much respect for it, and himself, to go to such extremes. He guessed he would just have to bear the loss, but it galled him.

A pale sun shone, silvering the soil of the freshly ploughed fields and burnishing the gold of the birch trees, and gradually, as he had hoped, the beauty of the morning and the autumn landscape began to smooth away his annoyance. He knew it was only a brief interlude of calm in the weather. The days were growing shorter, the nights cooler, but still warm turbulent air brought sparkling showers of rain, keeping the rivers swollen and the land frost free.

The fishing season was over, at least on the river, as the salmon and sea trout gathered in the tributaries in readiness for spawning. Anglers still came to his lakes, for the rainbow trout did not spawn and so did not lose condition, but this morning he was seeking a few hours of solace and relaxation.

He was making what was for him an annual pilgrimage, a brief interlude in which to watch the running fish ascend the river.

Half an hour later he pulled the car off the road a few yards from where a bridge spanned the river. Another car stood parked nearby, but he paid it little heed, for the path by the river was a favourite with walkers. He set off across the fields, close to the river bank, enjoying the faint warmth of the sun and the freshness of the morning air. Here the river was narrower, swifter flowing, cutting a deep channel through the gritty loam, and ancient alders lined the banks, binding the soil and providing food and shade for the trout. Here and there mushrooms glowed pearly white in the grass, brought to fruition by the warm rain and sun, and a few late blackberries glistened darkly in the light.

Three fields away the character of the land and the river changed completely. The pasture land gave way to a steep sided gorge, its flanks clad in rugged oaks. Instead of flowing silently over golden sand the river chattered over water-worn rock, foaming and splashing as it raced on its way into the placid waters of a wide pool, where the river was dammed by a high weir.

For centuries mankind had built such weirs, harnessing the power of the river to provide energy – for grinding corn, driving the machinery for cotton and woollen mills, and latterly to generate electricity. Often they built the weirs too high, forming barriers over which the spawning fish could not pass. Since salmon were considered a cash crop, to be harvested annually the same as wheat or hay, fish passes had been built into the weirs in a series of steps which the fish could climb with more ease.

The mill had long gone, burned down in a fire which broke out one windy May night over a century before, but the weir remained, almost as solid and steadfast as when it had been built. It was to this spot that Martin made his way, hoping for a sight of the fish leaping up through the foaming white water of the pass. Slightly to his dismay, he saw as he approached that he was not alone. Another figure stood there, a woman with an elfin face and dark hair. She flickered a smile of greeting as he drew near, but for a moment he thought he saw a look of annoyance there. She had strange eyes, he thought, golden, like those of a cat. Maybe a witch, a water sprite, only he didn't think naiads wore jeans and a battered old jacket. A substantial sprite, he thought, grinning back as his eye took in the curves of her figure.

Neither one spoke. Conversation in any case would have been impossible above the roar of the water foaming over the weir. Martin perched himself on a low rock and settled down to wait her out. Few people, in his experience, had the patience or interest to linger more than ten minutes. He stared down at the swirling brown water below the fall, waiting for a fish to break surface. Suddenly one came, a shimmering silver bar, a flicker of movement in the sun before it vanished again. Another and another followed in quick succession, one arched in a silver crescent, another ramrod straight, its tail quivering with the effort. These were sea trout, fish of around two or three pounds in weight, and he thought half wistfully of the fight they would have given him if he had hooked them on a fly one July night. Still, they would return another year, bigger and stronger, and perhaps he would be waiting for them.

There came a lull, something that Martin knew happened, although he was at a loss to explain it. For a few hectic minutes the river would be alive with leaping fish, and then there would be an interlude during which nothing happened. Yet in the course of a few hours he would see more fish going over the weir than he had caught all season. It was reassuring to him, this sign of plenty, and one of the main reasons why he made his pilgrimage. Today the air was calm and the sun warm, so waiting was no penance, but in previous years he had sat watching in a biting east wind, on into the dusk of an autumn evening.

Now a big fish broke surface, a salmon of some ten pounds or more, scorning the easy way up the fish pass and leaping straight at the solid rampart of the weir. Twice it fell back and tried again, this time hanging on the sill of the weir for long, agonising seconds, before sliding forward into the safety of the pool beyond. From beside him came a faint cheer, and he realised with a start that the woman was still there, standing statuesque beside the weir, her face alight with pleasure, her small hands applauding wildly. She grinned at him like a little child, and he waved back, sharing her delight at the salmon's success.

With a start he realised she had been standing there without moving for over half an hour. She reminded him of a Navajo girl he had once seen, standing staring rapt over the Grand Canyon in Arizona. It had made him dizzy just to watch her poised above the awesome chasm below, yet she had seemed oblivious to the danger. He frowned. Just watching the swirling current could cause vertigo, and a fall on these rocks could be serious, if not fatal. All the same he felt constrained not to interrupt her reverie.

Instead he returned his gaze to the water, watching as at intervals fish went by. Some moved through swiftly and surely. Sometimes there was drama, as when a fish fell back time after time, or beached itself among the rocks in its eagerness to climb the weir. Once there was humour, as a little brown trout wriggled its way up without effort. It seemed after a while that the legions of fish were so numerous they were beyond counting, but Martin knew that this was not the case. Indeed their numbers had dwindled in the past decade. Net fishing on the high seas and in the estuaries, disease and pollution in the rivers, poaching and predation, had all taken their toll, and now it seemed mankind was harvesting the very food the fish depended on. Martin had heard somewhere that over a million tons of sand eels, prime food for both salmon and sea trout, had been taken from the North Sea in one year. The Danes were even using the oil from the eels to fuel power stations. He winced at the thought, trying to visualise a million tons, and failing.

He felt a slight twinge of guilt and remorse as it occurred to him that some of the sand eels had been made into fish food which had gone to raise his rainbow trout. Then it occurred to him that in tolerating the osprey that was visiting his lake he was recycling some of those sand eels back into their proper place in the wild. Suddenly, ridiculously, he felt happier, more light-hearted, and he knew there would be no more thoughts of shot-guns and money lost.

He was so lost in his reverie that he did not notice the woman had moved until she was standing beside him. Her words were lost in the roar of the tumbling water, but she was waving a thermos flask, and obviously offering him a drink. His leg was stiff and aching through contact with the cold hard rock, and he welcomed the chance to move. He stood up, pointing up the hill to where a rustic wooden bench stood beside the path, and led the way there. Nicola followed, still wondering, as she had been on and off since she had first set eyes on the stranger, why he should seem familiar to her. 'Tall and dark, walks with a limp. A heron.' Suddenly she had it, the man Paul had spoken of, the man who ran the trout fishery, Martin Collier.

The coffee was hot and strong, heavily sweetened just the way he liked it, and he sipped it gratefully. The roar of the water over the weir was now but a soft murmur, and the silence seemed to settle round them like a thick warm cloak. Somewhere high in the trees a robin sang his territorial song, a thin, high, reedy piping which carried undertones of faint melancholy, foretelling winter and hard times to come. More comforting was the low call of the woodpigeons from the oaks.

His coffee finished, Martin was about to introduce himself, when Nicola held up her hand. 'Don't tell me. I know who you are, or at least I think I do. Let's see if I am right.'

Martin blinked when she told him. 'But how . . .?'

Swiftly she explained, carefully omitting the bit about the heron.

Martin nodded. 'Yes, I know Paul. He's a good fisherman, not just skilful, but caring too. Not like some of the slobs you meet.' He hesitated a moment, frowning in remembrance. 'Then you must be Mrs Frayle, Nicola Frayle. You lost your husband tragically, a short while back? I'm sorry.'

Nicola shrugged, biting her lip. 'Life goes on.'

They sat in silence for a while, and then abruptly Martin asked, 'Do you fish?'

Laughing, Nicola shook her head. 'I wouldn't know one end of a fishing rod from another. I've enjoyed watching the fish, though. Paul told me it was a fascinating spectacle, and he was right.'

Silence fell between them again, but it was a companionable one, as each relived the events of the morning, Nicola recalling the extra piquancy of small pleasures shared, Martin less easy, acutely aware of her presence, the fragrance of her perfume, the rustle of her clothing as she moved, the burnished gleam of her hair.

Abruptly Nicola produced a pack of cigarettes from her pocket. Martin shook his head as she offered them, instead producing a rather battered old briar. 'I prefer this if you don't mind, but it's best if I stay to windward.'

Nicola watched the blue smoke curl lazily upward. 'My husband didn't approve. I still feel guilty.' She glanced sideways at him as she spoke. 'Forgive me, but you looked like a man with a problem when you arrived, but now you seem to have resolved it. Am I right?'

Martin nodded, staring down at the river. 'Not so much resolved it, as learned to live with it, I suppose.' Then he told her about his visitor. 'Just sitting here now it seems so petty, complaining about a bird taking a few fish, but it was really beginning to bug me.' He looked at her, suddenly alarmed by her expression. 'What's the matter? Have I said something to distress you?'

Nicola took a long time putting out her cigarette and burying the stub under a patch of moss. 'It's not what you've said. It's what I've done.' Then she told him her side of the story. 'So you see, it's all my fault.'

To her intense relief, Martin began to laugh. 'Isn't it a small world, though? But you mustn't blame yourself. If it's anyone's fault, it's the poachers who set the damned net in the first place.'

'You're too charitable,' said Nicola. 'That wretched bird has caused nothing but trouble and aggravation ever since I found it. I really am sorry.' She looked at her watch. 'Look, I really must go. I've stayed too long as it is. I'll leave you in peace, and I hope the osprey will soon do the same.'

Suddenly he was reluctant to lose her company. 'It's late for me too. I'll walk back across the fields with you if you don't mind.'

They set off towards the cars. Several times Martin began to say something, and then changed his mind. Only when they were in the lane did he speak. 'Look, if you'd like to see your protégé again, please do call. He comes early in the morning I'm afraid, but you're welcome. In fact you're welcome any time.'

'Thank you,' said Nicola. 'Thank you. I'd like that.' But she was careful not to commit herself to a specific date.

There were times when Nicola felt she was possessed by a malevolent black imp which sat inside her skull, just behind the bridge of her nose, peering out at the world through her eye sockets, and trying to control her will. Most of the time he lay sleeping, but occasionally he would awake and try to interfere. This was one of those occasions.

By the time she reached home she had decided not to take Martin Collier up on his invitation, but that afternoon she found herself looking up his telephone number, just in case she should change her mind. She was immediately aware that the imp was awake. 'Why should I bother?' she asked herself.

'Because you're bored out of your skull,' said the imp. 'You have been since the osprey left.'

'Which is a very good reason for not phoning him,' Nicola answered. 'I don't know the guy. I'm not even sure I want to know him, and I doubt if we have anything in common, in fact I don't even know if I like him.'

'How will you ever find out, if you don't contact him?' enquired her tormentor.

'Shut up!' snapped Nicola. 'Anyway, you are right about one thing. I'm bored, and the best cure for boredom is work.' So ignoring the fine layer of dust that seemed to have settled everywhere in the house she attacked the garden, clearing out the greenhouse and preparing the bench ready for the half hardy plants that needed protection from the winter. She dug over the ground left vacant in the vegetable plot and then attacked the potting shed, washing the plant pots and grading them in their respective sizes, turfing out the debris of broken seed trays, empty plastic bags and bits of twine that had accumulated during the summer. Then she cleaned and sharpened the tools, wincing at the thought of David's fury if he could see the state they were in. When they were dry she gave them a coating of oil and hung them all on their allotted hooks, instead of throwing them into a corner as usual. At night she went to bed early, taking a large gin with her, and slept soundly until morning.

Over the next two days she found her resolution wavering. On three occasions she was on the point of telephoning Martin Collier, once getting as far as dialling the number. Each time, at the last moment, she heard the imp sneering at her, causing her to slam down the receiver in a fury. Then, on the third day, the phone rang. She had just finished in the garden, and her hands were covered in oil and grime. She picked up the receiver between finger and thumb and held it to her ear. It was Mary, from the farm, and from the sound of her voice she was in a state bordering on desperation. 'Nicola. Where have you been all day? I've been trying to reach you. Listen: will you come to dinner tonight? Paul has invited that fellow from the trout fishery and I need you to make up a fourth.'

'Its out of the question,' said Nicola firmly.

'Oh please,' wailed Mary. 'Please come. I'll be bored out of my mind otherwise. You know what they're like. They'll talk fishing and shooting all evening, and I won't get a word in edgeways.'

'My hair is full of mud, blood and beetles, my hands are like a dishwasher's, I've a long scratch down one arm, and I've laddered my last pair of tights,' said Nicola. 'Anyway, I don't feel sociable.'

'You don't need to be,' said Mary. 'They probably won't notice you're there after the first five minutes.'

Nicola raised her eyes to the ceiling. 'That's different. Well, thank you Mary. You certainly know how to reassure a girl!'

'Do I?' asked Mary innocently. 'That's settled then. See you at seven-thirty,' and she hung up before Nicola could think of a suitable reply.

Slowly she replaced the receiver on the rest and turned to wash her hands. Was it her imagination, or did she hear inside her head an evil chuckle of glee?

Upstairs in the bedroom she surveyed the ruin reflected in the full-length mirror. The scratch she could do nothing about, but the rest of the wreck was just about worth salvaging, if she worked hard. The bit about the tights had been true, but she remembered that tucked away in a drawer she had a pair of pure silk stockings she was saving for some special occasion. She would wear them tonight, purely as a morale booster.

Two hours later she studied the results of her labours. She wore a simple gold dress, and gold high-heeled sandals. An amber necklace reflected the colour of her eyes, and her dark hair shone like a raven's wing. The stockings added just the right finishing touch, dark, sleek, and somehow slightly sinful. She gave a small smirk of satisfaction. Of one thing she was certain: both men would notice her, and it would serve Mary right if she was the one who was ignored.

Her preparations had made her ten minutes late, and it was Mary who greeted her at the door, wearing a simple but stylish green jump suit. 'I thought you said you hadn't got a pair of tights,' she said, glaring accusingly at Nicola's legs.

'I'm not wearing any,' said Nicola, raising the hem of her dress.

Mary snorted. 'Don't you dare flash those legs at Paul,' she hissed. 'I won't be able to control him for a week.'

Nicola giggled, and looked around. There was no sign of either of the two men. 'What have you done with him anyway?'

'Oh, it's as I warned you. He's built himself a new cold smoker in the wash house. Fitted an old refrigerator and a length of drainpipe above a disused copper boiler. I'm surprised he hasn't blown us all to kingdom come. He couldn't wait to show it off to Martin.'

The sound of voices interrupted her. 'You see, the secret of cold smoking is keeping the temperature just right. Too hot, and the fish dries out. Too cold, and the fish won't cure. That's where the insulation of the fridge ...' Paul's voice trailed off as he came into the room and caught sight of the vision that confronted him. He stood gaping, his large frame completely blocking the doorway. 'Nicola,' he stammered. 'You're ... You're looking well.'

'If you'll just get out of the way,' said Mary. 'I'll introduce Martin.'

His hand was cool and dry, and it held hers not a moment too long. First impressions count, thought Nicola, and warmed towards him. She had seen his pupils widen at the sight of her, and knew she too had scored full marks.

'Actually, we've already met,' said Martin, as Paul served them with drinks. 'Didn't Nicola tell you?'

'Mary rang off this afternoon before I had the chance,' said Nicola sweetly. 'I expect she had something cooking.'

Hastily Martin explained how they had met at the waterside.

'You went, then?' said Paul to Nicola, his eyes suddenly alight. 'Isn't it an incredible spectacle? You know, I reckon that if a man had a private stretch of river and charged admission, he'd make quite a nice living.'

'Bit seasonal, though,' hazarded Martin. 'You might only see the fish running about twice a year.'

Paul looked crestfallen, but then brightened up. 'Ah! But you don't tell the punters that. Just tell them they've been unlucky, and to come back again. They'd still think they'd had their money's worth.'

'I certainly did,' said Martin. 'The company, and the coffee, were an added bonus.'

Nicola sat back and raised her glass to him, and without realising it crossed her legs. Seeing this Mary hustled Paul away into the kitchen, leaving them alone together.

They sat in silence for a few moments. Despite his outward composure, Martin felt suddenly ill at ease. The rather chubby chrysalis he had met at the riverside, swathed in jeans and layers of wool and nylon, had metamorphosed into a very glamorous creature indeed. He felt totally captivated, not only by the curves of her figure, but by the colour of her eyes, and the way her mouth moved as she smiled, or drank. Suddenly he realised he was staring. 'You like solitude then?' he asked.

Nicola nodded. 'Don't get me wrong. I enjoy good company, but I don't crave it every minute of the day.' She frowned, remembering her desire to share small moments of delight with someone of like mind, but it was too early for revelations of that nature yet.

'I know what you mean,' said Martin. 'In fact I find I need time to be alone every day. Without that interlude I soon start to get tetchy.' He smiled wryly. 'It wasn't always easy

66

to find in the army. Now I seem to be blessed with a surplus.'

'There's a difference, isn't there,' said Nicola, 'between the solitude you seek, and that which is thrust upon you?'

Martin nodded slowly, aware of her recent widowhood, not wanting to be insensitive. 'All the difference,' he said. 'The difference between sweet and bitter.'

The sound of muffled thumping came from the kitchen, and a moment later Paul emerged, looking hot and flushed. 'Mary's trying the best of three falls with a steak,' he announced cheerfully. 'I'd hate to be that butcher when she catches up with him. Still, if they're too tough we'll mince them and have a cottage pie. More drinks anyone?'

Despite Paul's prognostications, the steaks were delicious, tender and juicy, and Paul produced an excellent Chilean wine to go with them, smooth and velvety. Between them Nicola and Mary managed to keep Paul off his favourite subjects of fishing and farming, and the atmosphere was relaxed and pleasantly companionable. Martin proved highly knowledgeable about music, and entertained them with one or two extremely funny stories about the more bizarre aspects of service life. He seemed to harbour no bitterness about his injury or early retirement. Indeed Nicola got the impression that he had gone through his career standing slightly apart from his fellow officers and men, playing the role of observer rather than active participant.

Independently, Mary came to the same conclusion. Observing him throughout the meal, she realised that his share of the conversation was kept to the absolute minimum required of courtesy. Instead he seemed engrossed in Nicola, watching every movement of her hands and face, drinking in every detail of her appearance, as if storing it in memory for future use.

'There's a man that's smitten,' she remarked to Paul as they settled to sleep.

'Bit early for matchmaking, isn't it, woman?' grunted Paul.

'It's never too early,' purred Mary happily, slipping her hand round his waist. 'Did you notice Nicola's legs?'

'Can't say I did,' replied Paul.

'Liar,' said Mary, and then Paul drew her into the crook of his arm, and they forgot about neighbours for that night.

Chapter Eight

A couple of days after the dinner party Martin rang Nicola, repeating his invitation to come and see the osprey, and suggesting she join him for breakfast the following morning. So Nicola found herself in the strange position of enjoying a rather good kedgeree in a man's bedroom, beside the big picture window that overlooked the lakes.

She was enchanted with the view, having somehow expected something more artificial, more tawdry in a way, yet how she could not quite define. The lakes seemed to have settled into the landscape as if they had lain there for centuries rather than just a couple of years, and Martin had been so careful with his landscaping and planting that nothing seemed too ornamental or out of place. 'How do you like living in Devon?' she asked.

Martin swallowed a mouthful of coffee. 'Loving every minute,' he replied. 'It's been the fulfilment of a dream. Though of course I was born and raised on the coast, only a few miles from here.'

Nicola raised her eyebrows. 'I didn't realise,' she said. 'Neither Paul nor Mary ever said anything.'

'I don't suppose they knew,' laughed Martin. 'Paul usually prefers to talk about fish, rather than boring subjects like people.'

'So do your parents still live around here?' asked Nicola.

Martin shook his head. 'My father died before I was born. That's his photo over there on the wall.'

Nicola studied the portrait of a rather younger version of Martin, dressed in the uniform of an officer in the Second

World War. 'Good Heavens!' she exclaimed, and then blushed. 'I wondered why you had a picture of yourself. What happened?'

'He was killed in action in Korea,' Paul explained. 'That picture, and a few medals, is all I have of him. My mother never remarried. Instead she devoted her life to the British Legion, helping those, as she put it, less fortunate than her man, who at least died instantly, rather than having to endure a lifetime of pain and suffering.'

He chuckled. 'Such high-flown principles didn't stop her from enjoying a full social life. Still don't, in fact. She lives in a flat in Bayswater, the merriest widow in town. I visit her occasionally, but I can't stand London for long.' He laughed again. 'Some of my earliest memories are of a succession of uncles from my boyhood, some of whom I'm still firm friends with, who were always extremely circumspect in their coming and going, and very generous to a fatherless boy.'

He attacked his kedgeree, having got somewhat behind with talking. 'It was I suppose taken for granted that I would follow my father into the marines. Certainly no other career was ever considered, either by my mother or me.'

Nicola pondered this a moment in silence. 'Yet I would have thought, having lost a husband, that a soldier's life would be the last thing she would want for her son.'

'Oh, quite the opposite,' said Martin. 'She used to say we could always remember him with pride. "Age shall not weaken them." That sort of thing. Better to die young, suddenly, unexpectedly, in a moment of rage, savage joy, or even terror, than moulder into senile old age.' He paused, and began to butter a slice of toast, thickly, meticulously, smoothing down the edges as if he'd said nothing out of the ordinary.

Nicola sat, her breakfast forgotten, trying instead to digest this alien philosophy. 'And you go along with that?' she queried. It seemed to her that not only was it a glorification of war, but a very small step from convincing yourself you were doing the other guy a favour by shooting him.

Martin looked up at her and grinned sheepishly. 'Oh yes. Absolutely. It's funny, as a boy, I was fascinated by the lives of Red Indians, Plains Indians, only my interest went deeper than most boys. Still does as a matter of fact. Their mothers used to pray daily that their sons would die bravely in battle. Old age and cowardice were the things to fear, not death itself. The warriors themselves had a saying . . . "A good day to die." In view of which . . .' He paused, and smiled sardonically. 'It's rather ironic, isn't it, in view of all that? I end up wounded, but not likely to die, and here I am enjoying my retirement twenty years before it is due.'

'Does your leg give you much trouble now?' asked Nicola.

'Aches a bit after a hard day,' Martin admitted. 'But things could be a lot worse. I could have lost the leg.'

'Or been killed?'

Martin shrugged. 'I don't know the answer to that one. What you don't have you don't miss, and all that. But I wouldn't have had this, and I wouldn't have got to meet you.'

Nicola flushed, and buried her nose in her coffee. It was the first time he had acknowledged he found her attractive. She sat without speaking, trying to reconcile the slim, dark, almost dapper man who sat opposite with his beliefs. It was hard to conceive he may have killed, to imagine him as dangerous or cruel, yet she had to admit that the notion added to his attraction. He was so utterly unlike David. He was, she supposed, an anachronism, born out of his time. He should have been a Mongol warrior, a Comanche brave, a Tuareg chief. In which case, she thought, he would probably have been smelly, and even verminous. Maybe he was just a little boy who never grew up, any more than his girl mother had.

It was full daylight now, and the sun rising behind the leafless trees cast long shadows across the lake. From time to time, as he was talking, Martin's eyes flickered towards the window, and suddenly he reached over and grasped Nicola's wrist. 'Look,' he whispered.

Nicola half turned to look out of the window, just in time to see the osprey glide in over the lake. As she watched it circled once, hovered briefly and dived, to emerge shaking itself like a dog, in a shower of spray that sparkled in the sun. It must have missed its prey, for its talons were empty, but on the second attempt it surfaced clutching a bar of silver that flapped frantically in the cold air. Next moment the osprey had vanished, and Nicola released a long pent up breath. It was the first time she had seen her protégé in action, and she felt a glow of satisfaction at being instrumental in its survival, even if it was robbing Martin of his precious fish.

'Oh!' she breathed. 'That was magnificent. I'm so glad I came. Thank you for asking me, and thank you for not harming him, even though he is robbing you blind.'

'Thank you for coming, ma'am,' said Martin. 'I admit I thought of shooting him, but the death penalty is a bit harsh for petty theft, and anyway I couldn't bring myself to shoot a fellow angler. I'm glad I didn't now.'

Suddenly Nicola realised he was still holding her by the wrist. She made no effort to withdraw it, and as their eyes met she felt a desire to know more about this gentle warrior who had come into her life. At that moment a car door slammed, and they heard the sound of male voices. Martin jumped to his feet with a start. 'Customers,' he announced. 'I'd forgotten all about them. I'd better go and let them in.'

Left to herself, Nicola began to clear the breakfast table. The moment of intimacy had passed, and the reality of the day was beginning. A few minutes later Martin returned. 'Sorry about this,' he said. 'I can't leave these duffers on their own. One of them is bound to fall in. Look, I've got a blank day coming up. If it's fine, come up on the moor with me. I may be able to show you something interesting. If you'd like to, that is.'

Intrigued, Nicola agreed.

A few days later she lay on a shelf of weather worn granite, peering down into the water. The current flowed in a long, glassy glide over golden gravel, scoured clean of weed and moss, and here the fish lay, long, lean torpedo shapes, glowing softly pink in the morning light. From where she lay she could count six hen fish, each with her retinue of waiting males. The cock fish were now grotesque caricatures of the slim silver fish that had emerged from the sea, their bodies emaciated, ulcerated and scarred from fighting among themselves, and from the battering they had received from the rocks on their journey upstream. Their lower jaws were elongated and deformed into ugly twisted beaks. Their backs were black, their flanks a dirty red, their once silver bellies grey and yellow.

The salmon were spawning. Some had spent the long days of summer idling in deep, dim, cavernous pools below the river banks, where alder roots twisted and twined like serpents in torment, and the light was green and cool. Here they sheltered between water-worn granite boulders which had lain undisturbed on the river bed since before the ice age, waiting as their bodies transformed energy and protein and fat into ripening ova. Others had joined them, forging their way up from the sea, and together they had braved the swollen brown waters of the autumn spates, coming at last to rest in the clear cold head waters of the tributaries, high on the windswept moors.

Most of the cock fish were smaller than the hens, but one was a massive brute, perhaps weighing as much as twenty pounds, lying alongside the largest of the hens, a fish of about the same weight. As she watched, Nicola saw him turn and strike with savage fury at one of the smaller cocks, driving him away from the female in a flurry of action faster than the eye could follow. Next moment he was back, lying alongside, and slightly to the rear of the hen.

As if reminded of her duties the hen fish suddenly turned on her side and forged upstream, vigorously flapping her broad, fan-like tail. This action disturbed the gravel, which was forced downstream, aided by the current, to form a small heap. The hen fish paused momentarily and then dropped back, hovering and sinking so that her vent covered the hollow thus formed. Suddenly she quivered violently, and a stream of orange-pink eggs spurted from her. Simultaneously the male shook in a spasm of ecstasy, and the water was briefly clouded with white milt. A few eggs which escaped fertilisation drifted away downstream, to be snapped up by a waiting brown trout, who had stationed himself in readiness for that event.

Again the process was repeated. Again the hen fish cut a trough in the gravel, and the displaced pebbles drifted down to bury the eggs already laid. So it would continue, until the trough, the redd, was nearly a yard long, and the female was spent. Nicola sighed and stretched. Although the sun was warm on her back the granite rock was icy cold, and she suddenly realised she was ravenously hungry. Beside her Martin sat, his knees drawn up to his chin, his pipe cold in his hand. He had not spoken or moved since they had arrived, and still he sat, motionless as a graven image, his whole attention so rapt and intent on the fish that she hesitated to break his reverie. Instead she rested her eyes on the rugged splendour that lay spread before her.

Earlier in the day, when the hoarfrost still lay thick on the ground, they had driven up through the valley, climbing up past the oak woods, past the patchwork of tiny fields, along the network of winding lanes where thatched cottages nestled like broody hens beside the verge, to the high moors. It was one of those rare December days when weather and climate conspired to bring out the full beauty of the winter landscape. Frost still lingered in the sunless hollows, but the sun shone out of a clear blue windless sky, and a million diamond dewdrops clung to the wine-red branches of the leafless birches. The rolling moor stretched out before her, the bracken faded now to bronze, the sear grasses ivory yellow and russet red, the grey granite rocks daubed with lichens, red and yellow and black, like redskins in their war paint. Wild ponies picked delicately at the growing tips of the wind bitten gorse, and sheep cropped the sparse grass between the boulders. The only sound was the soft murmur of the stream, and the harsh croak of a distant raven, a tiny tear in the fabric of the silence.

Suddenly, with a speed that startled her, Martin sprang to his feet. 'I'm hungry,' he announced. 'Are you?'

Nicola nodded, and was about to rise to her feet when he held up a hand. 'Wait here,' he commanded. 'I've got some stuff in the car. I won't be more than a few minutes.' Then he was gone, jogging away down the track with a curious rolling gait that seemed slow, but which rapidly carried him out of view. Nicola returned her gaze to the river, but after a few moments her attention wandered. If the truth were told she had been looking forward to the cosy atmosphere of a country pub, with a warming drink and hot soup beside a blazing log fire.

She did not have to wait long before Martin reappeared, carrying a large rucksack and a travelling rug. Squatting down beside a large rock, he spread the rug on the turf, and rather like a magician pulling rabbits out of a hat, began to empty the rucksack of its contents. There was whisky in a flask, and a bottle of sparkling mineral water to dilute it. There was hot onion soup in a thermos flask, crusty rolls, hard-boiled eggs, salt, pepper, a slice of brie, apples, and a bottle of Côtes du Rhône. Glasses, plates, cutlery and napkins completed the spread.

Nicola was impressed, and said so. Martin shrugged. 'They didn't make me leader of the Eagle patrol for nothing,' he joked. '"Be prepared," is the motto.' He poured whisky into the glasses and began to add mineral water. 'Say when.'

Nicola leaned back against the rock. 'What happens now?'

Martin looked faintly perplexed. 'I thought we'd eat, unless . . .'

Hurriedly Nicola enlightened him. 'No, I mean what happens to the salmon eggs? How long do they stay in the gravel? How soon will they grow into salmon?'

Martin swirled the amber liquid in his glass. 'It depends a bit on water temperature. The eggs will lie snug and safe in crevices in the gravel, washed by clean cold water and safe from winter floods and predators. Only severe frost can harm them. In about a month it is possible to distinguish the eyes, and in about ninety to a hundred days the little fish emerge. If the water is cold from snow melt it takes a bit longer, but if the winter has been mild the whole process is speeded up. It's rather neat really. The whole process is timed so that the young salmon emerge just as the rest of life is burgeoning round them. If they emerge too soon, there's no food. If they leave it too late, there's less time for them to make optimum growth before the next winter.

'The infant fish are called alevins, and at this stage they are little more than a pair of goggle eyes and a pink tail attached to a yolk sac that was the egg. They stay like this for about a month, until the yolk sac is fully absorbed, and then they become free swimming fry, emerging from the gravel into the big bad world ... Then they are really up against it. They are prey to dragonfly larvae, water beetles, trout, eels, kingfishers, goosander, merganser, herons, cormorants, even their own kind. But if they stay lucky, they will grow into what are called parr, little fish two or three inches long, very like trout, but with markings like fingerprints along their sides.'

He paused for breath, and began to pour the soup. 'How many eggs does a salmon lay?' asked Nicola.

'Oh, about six hundred for every pound of its body weight,' said Martin. 'So that big female there, say she weighs twenty pounds, she'll lay maybe twelve thousand eggs. Some fish may have up to nine hundred eggs per pound, but they are exceptional. However many they lay, only a tiny percentage will survive to become mature salmon. Here, drink your soup while it's hot.'

Obediently, Nicola sipped the scalding liquid, as Martin continued. 'The parr stay in the river about two years, growing and feeding, until one April when they are about six or eight inches long, they assume silvery coats and begin the long journey down to the sea. Even then they are not safe. They are at the mercy of grey seal and gannet, of shark and tope and conger, pollack, cod, tuna, anything big enough and fast enough to catch them. Still, for the survivors it is all worth while, because the feeding in the sea is incredibly rich, and so they grow fast. Some may only stay at sea a year, to return to the river as grilse. Most stay two years, or maybe three.'

'Whereabouts in the sea do they go?' queried Nicola.

'For a long time nobody knew,' said Martin, 'but then, unfortunately, their feeding grounds off the Faroes and the waters south west of Greenland were located, and thousands of tons are now netted each year. Fortunately, salmon farming has reduced the value of these fish to the price of cod, so commercial fishing has grown less and less profitable. The worst threat to salmon and sea trout stocks now is the harvesting of the small fish that they feed on. Sand eels, for instance. Millions of tons scooped up to make animal feed, food pellets for farmed salmon, or even used as fuel for power stations. How short-sighted can you get?'

Nicola was studiously engaged in picking the shell off a hard boiled egg. 'I suppose some of that fish meal went into producing this?'

'That and millions of others, not to mention chickens, turkeys, pigs, livestock of all kinds.'

'Including your trout,' said Nicola mischievously.

Martin grinned. 'Including my trout. Which are rapidly disappearing inside an osprey, so nature is getting its own back in the end.'

For a while Nicola seemed fully preoccupied with her egg. Then she said, 'Many people would argue that our first duty is to provide cheap, wholesome food for the nation. We've spent years working towards that goal. Now that we've achieved it, it seems irrational to query the wisdom of it. After all, if we've got farmed salmon, we don't need the wild stocks, so it makes sense to use the food wild salmon would eat to feed the artificially reared ones. You are an angler. How can you convince non anglers that you are not merely acting out of self interest in wishing to preserve wild salmon? I mean, how do you persuade them it is in their interests too?' She took a long swig of wine, and blushed, suddenly aware she sounded exactly like David, playing devil's advocate while cross-examining a witness.

'Oh, easily,' said Martin. 'In the first place, if it wasn't for the self interest of anglers and riparian owners, salmon would have become extinct long ago. Poaching, pollution, abstraction, hydroelectric schemes, a host of factors would have seen to that. Secondly, even though we can raise salmon artificially, wild stocks represent a gene bank of incalculable value, which we would be stupid to throw away, since we never know when we might need it. And thirdly there's the economic aspect. If a netsman caught a ten-pound salmon, he'd be lucky to get twenty pounds for it on the open market. On the other hand, it's been estimated that salmon caught by rod and line fishermen can be worth up to a thousand pounds apiece, whatever their weight.'

'A thousand?' scoffed Nicola. 'How can that be?'

'Easy. Say four guys come down to Devon for a week's

fishing. Say two of them get a fish, the other two have a blank week. It's not unusual in salmon fishing. By the time they've paid for fuel, fishing permits, tackle, hotel bills, booze, and so forth, they can easily spend five hundred pounds apiece. That's two thousand . . . a thousand pounds a fish. More if they bring their families.'

'I see what you mean,' said Nicola. 'So what you are saying is, as far as the salmon is concerned, the anglers are the nice guys, the only nice guys.'

'If I were a salmon, I'm not sure whether I'd rather be caught by an angler, an otter, or an osprey, but yes, the anglers are the only ones who care. Out of self-interest if you like, but also out of respect, of admiration, of love, of a kind.'

Nicola flushed, as with a sudden feeling of horror she realised that while Martin had been talking she had drunk almost all the bottle of wine. Whether it was the wine, or the recollection of her dead husband, or the inexorable persistence with which Martin countered all her assertions, she wasn't sure, but she was beginning to feel distinctly nettled. From the role of pupil, she seemed to have progressed to that of prosecuting counsel, to that of the accused. Made to feel guilty, for God's sake! 'Oh, come on,' she snapped. 'I care, and so must thousands of others, individuals who, rather than merely regarding salmon as some sort of crop, feel that as a species they have as much right to life as any other life form, including man.'

Martin hesitated. He was astute enough to recognise the warning signs, but reluctant, at this stage, to drop the subject. What the hell, he thought. If the lady simply wants to salve her conscience, she'll get no help from me. 'Maybe the term "crop" is a bit insensitive,' he said cautiously, 'but the fact remains, the future of the salmon ultimately depends on this, a healthy population present each year on the spawning beds. Not too many, not too few. Too few, and there won't be enough spawn to perpetuate the race. Too many, and the latecomers will destroy the redds already laid down. Most of the adult fish are going to die anyway, ninety-five per cent of the females, and nearly all the males.'

He hesitated a moment. He had been about to point out

that one caring individual had just been taught the facts of the salmon's life by, of all people, an angler, but he decided that if the fact wasn't obvious, it would be a cheap way of scoring points. Instead he went on: 'Sure salmon have as much right to life as any other form of life, but if you are going to accept that argument, then it follows that man, as an indigenous species of this planet, also has a right – as much right as an otter, an osprey or a seal – to take a salmon, as long as it is purely for his own use, to savour, to enjoy, to enrich his experience of life.'

'Hum!' said Nicola. 'You wouldn't starve if you never caught another salmon in your life.'

'Nor would the others. The otter could eat eels, the grey seal cod, the osprey chub and dace.'

'Hum!' said Nicola again. In truth she was weary of the debate. The wine was all gone, the ruins of the picnic lay all around them. The sun was westering as the short day drew to a close, and the rock against which they leant cast a slantwise shadow across the turf, cutting between them. It was as if a barrier had been raised, a rift neither could cross. Never having fished in her life, never having had the slightest inclination to do so, she couldn't comprehend why anyone should be so fanatical in the sport's defence. She felt as if she had fallen into a morass, a mire from which she could not escape, and in her struggles succeeded only in sinking deeper. She felt, cautiously, for firmer ground. 'I've heard somewhere that salmon always return to the river of their birth. Is that possible?'

Oh yes,' said Martin. 'Not only possible. It's the only way, if you think about it, that the system could work. Otherwise every salmon in the Atlantic could take it into its head to swim up the same river. That one would be choked with fish, while the rest would be empty. No one knows quite how they find their way across the ocean – perhaps by electromagnetism, perhaps by the stars – but certainly, after one, two, or even three years at sea, they recognise their own river by the smell, however much it is diluted. They will even return to the same pool in which they hatched.'

'And then die,' said Nicola.

'Most of them, but some survive to spawn again. That big

female has probably spawned two or three times, but the only way to find out would be to take a scale reading. Size doesn't really enter into it. She could be younger than some of the smaller fish.'

He fell silent, and began, in a desultory fashion, to tidy away the remains of the meal. He sensed, somehow, that the outing was over, and it had not been the success he had hoped for. Inwardly he cursed himself for being so obsessive, so single-minded in his attitude. He had meant the conversation to be sparkling, light-hearted, not a monologue on fish. She must think him a dreadful bore. In fact there was no worse kind of a bore than a fishing bore. 'I'm sorry,' he said. 'I seem to have gone on a bit.'

'No, really,' said Nicola quickly. 'It was fascinating, and the picnic was lovely, but it is getting cold, and late.' She fell to helping him pack the picnic things. 'It's me who ought to apologise. I drank most of the wine.'

Martin grinned ruefully. 'I'm driving anyway. I've got to get you home safely.'

They turned to go, but he took one last glance back at the pool lit by the setting sun, at the salmon lying patiently on the redds. Their lives were fulfilled. Already they were dying, amid the rosy embers of the year.

Chapter Nine

The fires of autumn slowly died, and the short days of winter drifted by, wet and warm. Occasionally white frost rimed the meadows, lingering on into the afternoon, but always by evening it had thawed, even in the sunless hollows of the hills. Perhaps because of the mild weather, perhaps because the memory of his injury was too recent for him to trust his wing over long distances, Iasgair lingered on in the valley. He clung resolutely to his roost in the dead ash tree, claiming the surroundings as his territory, and driving away any intruder – buzzard or crow or prowling fox – that threatened to invade his privacy.

He still regularly visited the trout fishery, but when the high tides coincided with daylight hours he haunted the estuary, quartering the shallow water as it flowed over the mud flats in search of infant flounders and dabs. Fishing was not always easy in the closing month of the year. Apart from the resident brown trout and the occasional salmon kelt, the river was empty of fish, the sea trout having migrated back to the sea after their autumn spawning ritual. In addition the river was often swollen and turbid with rain, making it impossible to locate a fish. Even the estuary was largely devoid of life, apart from the baby flatfish. The great shoals of bass and mullet, mackerel and sea trout that frequented its waters were mostly absent, far away in the deep warm waters of the sea, and would not return until the spring. So it was the trout fishery which sustained him when all else failed, and without this it is unlikely that he would have lingered in the valley very long.

81

Throughout this time, even when the days were short and the weather cold and dank, anglers continued to flock to Martin's fishery, and frequently, when he went to unlock the gates at eight in the morning, he found several cars parked in the lane, their impatient occupants busy assembling their tackle so as not to waste a moment of their day. He charged high prices for a day's fishing. He limited each angler to three fish, and he limited the number of anglers on each lake. Yet still he found himself turning away latecomers, and began to insist on advance booking, the fishermen not seeming to care what the weather conditions might be on their allotted day.

To Martin, many of these still water anglers were a strange and alien breed. In the main they were young, affluent, and had invested heavily in tackle and equipment. They were extremely skilled at casting their many highly coloured flies and lures, and well informed on aquatic life in general, but their main preoccupation was with catching fish, the heavier the better, and an angler who had not bagged his limit at the end of the day tended to be disgruntled and surly.

Martin quickly got to know the fishmongers, as he called them, and after a while he began turning them away, claiming to be booked up, even though he knew he was losing money. Among the others, though, men who could always find the time to chat, who enjoyed the bird life that haunted the lakes, who remained cheerful and content even at the end of a blank day, who came again and again, he soon began to make firm friends.

As the days grew shorter and dawn came later, so the osprey was delayed in his fishing, and inevitably the time came when a quartet of anglers was assembled by the lakeside when he arrived. They were a mixed bunch. The oldest was a retired dentist. One was an accountant, another a coach driver, and the youngest a farm worker, but all were united in their love of angling, and had long been on first-name terms. They regularly fished together, and at lunchtime, or when sport grew slow, they gathered in the little hut Martin had provided for shelter, smoking and yarning and sometimes sharing a flask.

Now they watched in slack-jawed amazement as the osprey

circled the lake on slow flapping wings, hovered an instant and then dived, emerging in a silver shower of spray with a fat rainbow flapping in his talons. Nobody spoke until the great bird was lost to view among the trees. 'That's the way to do it, young Tom,' remarked the dentist.

'I didn't know there were any osprey in these parts,' said the accountant. 'I wonder if he is a regular visitor?'

'Collier would know,' said Tom.

'Suppose he doesn't,' said the dentist. 'Is it a good idea to tell him an osprey is robbing him of his fish?'

'Why not?' queried Tom.

'Because he might not take kindly to his fish being nicked,' replied the dentist. 'And he might be tempted to take the law into his own hands, with both barrels of a shotgun.'

'He'd never do that,' said Tom.

'You never know,' said the dentist. 'Personally, I think it is a case of least said, soonest mended. I vote we stay quiet about it.'

All this time the coach driver had remained silent. 'I've never seen anything like that in my life before,' he said at last. 'I'd as soon see that osprey catch a fish as catch one myself. I vote we keep quiet.'

So they agreed on a vow of silence, but unbeknown to them Martin had witnessed the whole episode from his bedroom eyrie. His heart sank as he envisaged his four best customers demanding their money back on the grounds that an osprey was ruining their fishing, and he was a little surprised to see the four disperse along the lake and start casting as if nothing untoward had occurred. So he decided to take the coward's way out, and leave the anglers undisturbed.

It so happened that sport on that particular morning was slow. The December day was mild and overcast, with no wind to ruffle the water, and it was almost lunchtime before a slight breeze rippled the surface and the first fish took. As it came to the net Martin decided he could delay making an appearance no longer, and sauntered slowly down to the lake. Here he was even more perplexed by the show of innocence that pervaded the air like a conspiracy. The fishermen talked about everything except ospreys, and at last he could stand the suspense no longer. 'I noticed you had a spot of competition earlier on,' he remarked quietly.

There was a moment's silence, and then the relief among the four was evident. 'Worth a day's fishing just to see something like that,' was the general opinion 'You ought to advertise,' said Tom. '"See the osprey." And charge for admission. The public will flock here.'

There was a general gasp of horror. 'Any more ideas like that young man,' growled the dentist, 'and we'll chop you into little pieces and feed you to the bird. If he'll eat you, which I very much doubt. I'm not sharing this lake with hordes of goggle-eyed spectators.'

So once again the four took a vow of silence, not to broadcast the news of the osprey's presence. Martin wandered off to find some lunch, totally bemused to find that his osprey was an asset to his fishery, rather than a liability as he had thought. He related his encounter to Nicola later that evening as he sat sharing her sofa, drinking strong black coffee and savouring a rather fine malt.

Several weeks had elapsed after the picnic before Nicola had decided to make amends for her boorish behaviour and invite Martin to dinner. She wanted to make a special occasion of it, so she set to work applying her somewhat neglected cooking skills in the kitchen, and taking inordinate care over the setting of the table before making herself as attractive as she knew how.

In deference to the time of year she had prepared tomato soup, followed by a steak and kidney pie, served with home-grown leeks and potatoes mashed in butter, and a lemon meringue. This, with the accompanying wine, had left them full fed and drowsy to the point of stupor, so it was a relief to move away from the table and into the cooler air of the living room.

When Martin had finished telling his tale about the osprey and the fishermen Nicola sat for a long while in silence, twirling the liquid in her glass and smiling softly to herself. 'You do care, don't you?' she said suddenly.

For some reason Martin felt slightly nettled. 'Care? Of course I care. Why shouldn't I?'

'Oh please, don't get me wrong. It's just that I was thinking. It seems that so many people say they care. In fact they rush around showing that they care, until something happens that affects them personally, and then suddenly it seems the only thing they care about is their own welfare.'

She took a sip from her glass and then set it down firmly. 'Whereas you. You just care. I mean, this wretched bird has caused you so much trouble and expense, even worry. And it would have been so easy for you to do something about it, quietly, one morning when no one else was about. And no one would have been any the wiser. Yet you didn't. I like that.'

Quite suddenly, and as much to her own amazement as Martin's, she burst into tears.

'Hey there,' said Martin gently. Quite unconsciously he slipped an arm round her shoulders, drawing her to him, while with the other hand he extracted a handkerchief from his breast pocket. Without a word she took it, and for a moment she rested her head where it lay on his shoulder, so that the perfume of her hair and the warmth of her prompted him to raise her chin and bend to kiss her lips.

She made no effort to resist, instead responding, leaning into him so that he felt the full firmness of her breasts against his chest. When at last they paused for breath she smiled up at him a little tremulously. 'I wanted to do that to you by the river,' he said quietly.

'And I wanted you to,' Nicola murmured. 'Instead I argued. You should have kissed me and shut me up.'

'I wasn't sure I could find you under all that wool.'

Nicola giggled. 'You might have had difficulty. I wonder how Eskimos manage?'

'They sleep naked under a pile of furs,' replied Martin, quite seriously.

Nicola felt a wave of sheer sensuous pleasure at the thought. 'Sounds like the ultimate in luxurious loving.'

With sudden shock she realised what she had just said, not merely the implication that they should make love, but amidst furs, dead animal skins! What would David have thought of her? With a sudden angry movement she thrust herself away, and sitting upright, she blew her nose loudly. 'I'm sorry,' she sniffed, 'but I was thinking of David, and, oh

85

dear!' She wept again, quietly, and this time Martin made no move to kiss her, but just sat, his arms around her, struggling desperately to control the emotions aroused in him by the close physical contact of her warm body.

Above all there was desire, so intense, so fierce that he was surprised at its strength, and a little afraid. His heart beat hard against his ribs, his mouth was dry, and he could feel himself trembling in every limb. There was also anger, that the spectre of the dead husband should make his presence felt in such a way, and frustration. He wanted nothing more than to throw her over his shoulder and carry her upstairs to the bedroom, but of course he couldn't. He could only sit there, a shamefaced idiot, like some schoolboy on his first date. He simply did not know what to do.

He was saved from any immediate decision by Nicola getting up and leaving the room. He poured himself another scotch, though part of him said it wasn't a very good idea, and sat back to ponder the situation. His experience with the opposite sex was limited in the extreme, and, he thought, hardly to his credit, confined as it was to occasional late night forays after the parties in the officers' mess had been wilder than usual. By tacit agreement, a man could not be held responsible for his behaviour under those circumstances.

This was different. It was not the fact that Nicola was still young enough and attractive enough to be very desirable, nor was it pity for a young widow in distress. Nor was it a reaction to the almost hermit-like conditions under which he had existed for the past two years. He had, he now knew, been building up to this confrontation for the past few months, as more and more she had come to occupy his thoughts and dreams. Now, it seemed, he had blown his chances, just like an impetuous kid.

Upstairs, Nicola sat at her dressing table, endeavouring to repair the damage to her make up. 'Silly cow,' she scolded herself. 'You've been wanting him to do that for weeks, and the moment he tries you shy away like a frightened virgin. Now he's probably given up and gone home, and you can't blame him.'

After a while she went downstairs. Martin was still sitting

where she had left him, and as she entered the room he stood up, facing her, irresolute. Quite deliberately she walked into his arms, and as they enfolded her she lifted her face to his. 'Sorry,' she murmured, 'I'm a neurotic little brat at times.'

His answer was soft and warm and lingering, and it was everything she had hoped for. She had read in magazine stories of women melting, eager, compliant, dissolving to liquid at a lover's touch. The desire she felt for this man was a maddening, burning itch she wanted raking away at all costs, swiftly, brutally, before it entirely consumed her. Yet still, somehow, she could not bring herself to lead Martin to the bed that she and David had shared for so many years. So, gently, but firmly, before events moved too far, and they both ended up in an undignified sprawl on the floor, she pushed Martin away. 'Not yet,' she whispered. 'But soon. I promise.' And with that, Martin had to be content for that evening.

Next morning Nicola woke with the memory of Martin's kisses still lingering about her lips. For a moment she lay, steeped in luxurious bliss, and then a shadow of remorse flickered across her mind, like a cloud sweeping over the sun. Refusing, even for one moment, to believe she had betrayed a man who was now dead, she got up, intending to banish all such thoughts from her mind.

She remembered she had promised to look out some old clothes for the church jumble sale, and she set about the task with a ruthlessness that soon produced a large pile of clothing and accessories, much of it David's – stuff she had been planning to dispose of for months, but which she had hesitated to touch for fear of the memories it would evoke. In rummaging through cupboards and drawers she came across his camera, unused since his death, a film only half exposed still inside.

She wondered idly what might be on the film. Not holiday snaps for sure. David was not given to such frivolity. Then she remembered why he had bought it. He had come home incensed one day, because a massive oak had been felled to make way for a road improvement scheme. 'It's vandalism,' he had exclaimed. 'Just think. It takes an oak the best part of a century to reach maturity, yet it can be cut down in an hour, logged up and sold for firewood in a day. Thousands of hours of stored sunlight squandered because it is suddenly fashionable to own a wood burning stove. Now there is nothing left but ash, and a memory. It's time someone kept a record of these trees, or future generations will be left wondering what our landscape looked like.'

So he had bought the camera. It had been expensive, she recalled, a single lens reflex with a bewildering array of stops and buttons and dials, but David had justified the extravagance by pointing out that film cost the same whatever the quality of the camera, and a picture was only as good as the lens that the light passed through. So he had set about making a pictorial record of all the trees in the neighbourhood, logging each one with a note of its species, height, girth, approximate age and locality.

It had become something of an obsession, because not content with a single portrait of the tree from its best angle, he had insisted on taking views from all four quarters of the compass. It then occurred to him that a tree, a deciduous one at any rate, changed with the seasons, so he began photographing the same tree in spring, summer, autumn and winter. It was ironic, she mused, that he should be cut down as swiftly and as savagely as one of his precious subjects.

He had taken only transparencies, and had never got round to buying a projector, instead using one at the university. After his death she had disposed of his papers, handing the relevant ones to various organisations and giving the rest, together with hundreds of transparencies, to the university archives. Now she wondered whether she ought to have this film processed, and if necessary send it on to go with the rest. Then suddenly, impulsively, she opened the camera and ripped the film out. Such things belonged to the past. From now on she intended to live for the present, and look forward only to the future.

There remained the question of what to do with the camera. She had no desire to take pictures of trees. Then it occurred to her that if she could learn to use it, she could perhaps take some pictures of the osprey at the trout fishery.

She bitterly regretted not having any record of his stay in the fruitcage. An instruction manual lay on the shelf beside the camera, and, jumble for the moment forgotten, she picked it up and began to study the pages.

That same afternoon she went out and bought half a dozen rolls of film, and proceeded to familiarise herself with the camera by taking snapshots of everything and anything in sight. The results of her efforts, not only with the first film, but the second and third, were so dismal that she began to despair of ever mastering the art, but gradually she overcame the problems of focusing and camera shake. She discovered that a picture had to be composed within the frame of the viewfinder, and that often a scene which was attractive to the human eye failed as a picture because of the limitations imposed by the lens. By the end of the week she was totally absorbed in her new hobby, and, though somewhat shaken by the amount of money she had spent, felt competent enough to try taking some photographs of the osprey in action.

Martin, who was secretly amused by Nicola's sudden fascination for her new interest, readily agreed to her coming over to the trout fishery early next morning, suggesting they have breakfast after the osprey had called. 'If he appears,' he warned her. 'He's not always reliable.'

The day dawned cool and bright, a brisk wind stirring the tops of the leafless trees. Nicola was by the lake before sunrise, shivering a little in spite of several layers of warm clothing, but determined to wait as long as need be. Time passed, clouds began to gather, and the rapidly changing light worried her a little. She had chosen the fastest exposure she dared, relying on the electronic sensor in the camera to choose the correct aperture, hoping that when the bird arrived her nerves would not fail her. Once a bird appeared out of the sun, startling her into action, but it was only a heron, which turned aside when it saw her.

Then, just as she was beginning to despair, the osprey appeared, and her shutter clicked time and again as he circled the lake before swooping down and taking a fish, far over near the opposite shore. Flushed with success she took one parting shot of the fish hawk disappearing among the trees, his prey clutched in his talons, and by now realising how cold and hungry she felt went in search of her breakfast.

Two days later a rather crestfallen Nicola handed Martin a package. Opening it he found a dozen prints, perfectly exposed and crystal clear, showing the trees, the lake, the sky, and in the middle of each one a small speck that might, or might not have been an osprey. The image was too tiny to distinguish detail. Martin sympathised as best he could, but at least he now knew what he could buy Nicola for Christmas.

Chapter Ten

Christmas came, and Martin, as he had planned, gave Nicola a telephoto lens for her camera. She had found a first edition of Henry Williamson's novel *Salar The Salmon*, a better book, in her opinion, than the much acclaimed *Tarka The Otter*. Both were delighted with their gifts, and between Christmas and the New Year Nicola was able to get more shots of the osprey.

On New Year's Eve Paul and Mary threw a party to which Martin and Nicola were invited, and as soon as Nicola got into the house Mary dragged her off into a corner. 'You managed to get that soldier fellah into bed yet?' she hissed.

'Really, Mary. You've got such a delicate way of expressing yourself,' murmured Nicola.

'Well, have you or haven't you?' insisted Mary.

'Well, no,' admitted Mary, 'but . . .'

'There are no buts,' insisted Mary. 'Get yourselves a dozen oysters and a pint of guinness and let nature take its course. Or do you both need hormone treatment?'

'It's difficult,' said Nicola desperately. 'It's . . . Oh, David still comes between us. I can't get him out of my mind.'

'Hmm,' said Mary. 'Better make that a pint of champagne.'

Then to Nicola's great relief more guests arrived, and Mary abandoned her to greet them.

Later in the evening Mary found a moment to have a word with Paul. 'She still hasn't bedded him yet,' she announced.

Paul blinked, opened his mouth to ask who she was

91

talking about, and then, guessing correctly, shut it again. Mary glared at him. 'A lot of help you're going to be, I can see.'

'What am I supposed to do?' asked Paul reasonably.

Mary thought for a moment. 'Get her smashed, and I'll send Martin up to put her to bed. That should do the trick.'

'I don't think that would work,' said Paul. 'Leave it to me. I'll think of something.'

Eventually he did, but it was not to be that evening, nor for some weeks to come.

At first January was fine and dry, but gradually a change came in the weather. An area of high pressure began to develop over the Arctic, and this grew in intensity, so that cold air began to spill down over Europe. Winds circling clockwise over the continent carried the cold across the North Sea and the Channel, so that at night the ground grew iron hard with frost, and high cloud by day kept the land from thawing.

As the peat bogs on the moor froze so the ground water was locked in chains of ice, and the river level dropped steadily lower. Ice formed near the shores, and the brown trout sank into deep water, lying comatose among the stones that littered the bed. Further north snow fell, and soon the skies were filled with migrant birds fleeing south to escape the cold – fieldfares, redwings, Scandinavian thrushes which had left their northern breeding grounds to seek sanctuary in the warmer climate of Britain, only to find it had betrayed them, pigeons, lapwings, waders, geese, and a host of smaller birds. Despite the intense cold, all these birds could survive as long as the land remained free of snow, which buried their food supplies and cut off their only source of energy and heat.

At first Iasgair ignored the cold. His dense mantle of plumage insulated him against the bitter chill, and he divided his time between the estuary and the trout farm. But, as the days passed, ice began to form over the lakes, and fringes of ice spread out over the mud flats of the estuary. Each day the cloud battalions continued to march silently and inexorably across the sky. The world was a monochrome of black and white and grey, and food grew steadily scarcer and harder to find.

Then, on an afternoon in mid-January, a deep depression, laden with moisture from the warm Atlantic, drifted slowly east to collide with the cold air sweeping across from the continent. The wind, which had been blowing steadily from the north east, veered south, losing its bitter chill so that for a while the air felt warm and damp. As the day drew to a close the wind dropped, the sky, overcast and heavy, took on a yellowish tinge, and just before dark the snow began to fall. At first the flakes were large and feathery, drifting down to touch lightly on every twig and leaf and grass blade, but as darkness fell the wind returned, and now the flakes were smaller, fragmented, swirling and dancing to the roar of the wind in the pines. Snow which had already fallen was whipped up off the fallow fields, piling in drifts against the hedgerows and across the lanes, and more snow fell to take its place, so that by dawn the world was buried in a muffling blanket of white. Yet still the snow continued to fall, swept across the sky by a strong south easterly wind.

By late afternoon the skies had begun to clear. A pale sun shone low on the horizon, and the blizzard had spent its might, though occasional snow flurries filled the air. Then darkness fell, and with it came the return of the frost. Iasgair woke to a world of white, and a silence so profound that the faint murmur of the river far below him seemed unnaturally loud. He shook his wings and lofted off the branch, flying slowly upstream, his wings lazily fanning the cold air, his eyes scanning the surface of the water in search of any movement beneath it.

The stream looked as dead and lifeless as the leafless trees. He climbed higher, passing swiftly over the arable land that lay between him and the estuary. Below him flocks of disconsolate birds huddled on the ground, their feathers ruffled against the cold. A large flock of fieldfares betrayed by the snow flew below him, urgently questing bare meadow land and finding none.

Down on the estuary the tide was running. Those mudbanks bare of snow held a shrilling concourse of birds, greenshank and plover, oyster catchers and curlew, stately white swans and gabbling brent geese. A heron stood at the water's edge, his dagger-like bill poised for instant action. The great bird stood so still he might have been graven in stone, but his yellow eye was alert for the slightest sign of life stirring in the cold water about his feet. A flock of dunlin rose in a whirr of wings as a peregrine falcon swept in amongst them, and one of their number died in an explosion of feathers. For the falcon at least there was no shortage of food.

Iasgair quartered the estuary, circling again and again, but no fish showed. Around noon, when the sun shone whitely through the mists of frozen vapour, he flew inland to try his luck at the trout fishery. Only one of the lakes had yet to freeze, and here ice claimed the greater part of it, leaving only a narrow channel kept open by the sluggish flow of the stream. Not a fish showed, and Iasgair returned to his perch in the ash tree, dozing through the short afternoon until darkness fell. That night he felt the cold for the first time.

As the temperature dropped small birds began to die, tiny sparks of life extinguished in the darkness and cold. Their frozen corpses littered the snow, where they were found by foraging foxes, so that by morning only the tracks of the foxes remained, crossing and recrossing the fields. Iasgair woke to a grey dawn, and a feeling of lassitude such as he had not experienced since he had fallen foul of the poacher's net. Hunger was beginning to sap his strength.

At this time of year he should have been basking in the sunlight of the tropics, quartering the low lying swamps of the Gambia, but the urge to migrate south had passed, obliterated in the trauma of his captivity, and the impulse to fly north was not yet on him. In any event he was too weak now to attempt a long journey, and unless he found food soon he would not survive very much longer. With his slow, ponderous flight, except when he was in a dive, and his specially adapted talons, he was ill equipped to capture prey other than fish. Indeed, he did not recognise small mammals and birds as a source of food, and it seemed that at last the instincts he had inherited from his forebears were about to betray him. For untold centuries evolution had passed the

94

ospreys by, for so successful had their lifestyle been that they had found no need to change, to adapt their ways.

Wearily Iasgair lofted off his perch and set off on another fruitless round of river, estuary and lake. The world was locked in chains of ice. Nothing stirred in the lifeless landscape. Even the wading birds seemed to have forsaken the estuary. In the late afternoon he passed over Nicola's garden, and something about the familiarity of the scene below made him circle in flight, and swoop down lower. Once, he knew, this region had been a source of food.

Despite the thick blanket of snow, he recognised the fruit-cage, and the block which still stood abandoned on the lawn. Nicola, ever one to procrastinate, had left things just as they were when he left, hoping at first that he might return, and then neglecting the task of clearing up in favour of more urgent chores. One of these, because of the bitter weather, was keeping a good supply of food available for the smaller birds.

Years ago David had hung a thick slab of elm wood on chains from the apple tree. Above it he had fixed a screen of wire netting designed to discourage the larger birds – rooks, magpies and seagulls – from pilfering the rations intended for songbirds. Neither of them had ever devised a way of discouraging starlings and squirrels, other than rushing outside and driving them away. Since a flock of starlings could empty the tray in minutes, this entailed frequent forays from the kitchen, and it was on one of these that Nicola espied the osprey circling the garden.

She stood for a moment in the snow, transfixed with delight that her protégé should have returned. Then she remembered she still had a few whiting left in the deep freeze. Here was one large bird she was only too happy to feed, so she darted back indoors, rummaged around in the freezer chest until she located the fish, popped it into her microwave, and switched the appliance to 'defrost'. The flesh would probably have the consistency of wet cotton wool, but under the circumstances she did not think the osprey would be too particular. The seconds dragged by as she waited impatiently, agonised by the thought that in the interval the osprey might well have flown away.

Without bothering to change her shoes she hurried up the garden path, sinking up to her knees in the unswept snow, and soaking the legs of her jeans. She need not have worried. The osprey sat huddled on top of the fruitcage, his wings wrapped around him and his head sunk on his chest. He made no move as she drew near, but merely watched as she brushed the snow off the old feeding block and laid the flabby corpse of the whiting on top. She retired to a safe distance and watched.

For a long time Iasgair sat motionless, unheeding, as though a meal of fish was the last thing in the world to occupy his mind. Then suddenly he raised his head. His great yellow eye blinked, and then he opened his wings and swooped down on the fish. There and then he tore it to pieces, holding the carcase down with one foot and gulping great gobbets of flesh, skin and bone. When all trace of the fish had vanished he looked around for a moment as if expecting more, and then flew inside the fruitcage through the open door, and settling on the perch composed himself to sleep.

Nicola stayed watching, knee deep in the snow. Her feet and legs gradually grew colder but she paid no heed. She scarcely dared to believe that her protégé, that she had nursed back to health so many months ago, should return when once again he was in need. Yet the evidence was there, right before her eyes. She wondered whether to shut the cage door on him, but then she realised that the answer to her question was academic, since the door was firmly wedged open with a snow drift, and any attempt to clear it would only disturb and perhaps panic him. Clearly, for the moment he had no intention of going anywhere, and doubtless he would be ready for another meal in a few hours' time. She turned back to the house, determined it would be ready for him when he awoke.

There were only two more whiting left in the deep freeze, and she was afraid more snow would come, binding her to the house without food for the osprey. Not even bothering to change her shoes, she got into her car and drove the three miles to the little market town near the coast. The highway department had managed to clear most of the snow, but the roads were rutted and icy, in places confined to a single lane, so that the trip took longer than she expected. The fishmonger had little to offer in the way of fresh fish, but she managed to get some more whiting and a few rainbow trout, wincing at the price, and thinking ruefully of the fat rainbows deep under the ice in Martin's fishery.

It then occurred to her that, having made the journey, it would be sensible to buy a few provisions for herself, so what with one thing and another it was nearing dusk as she fought the wheel of the little car the last few yards up the lane. As soon as she had unloaded her purchases she took one of the trout and hurried up the garden path with it, but the fruitcage was empty. Her bird had flown. She was cold and tired and wet and hungry, and she was near to tears as she laid the trout on the block and trudged back through the snow to the house, her feet like frozen blocks of ice. During the night an old dog fox, emboldened by hunger, entered the garden and found the trout. By now it had frozen to the block, but with teeth and claws he managed to tear most of the fish free. In the morning only a few shreds of skin and a scattering of bright silver scales showed where it had been.

Nicola found the remains at first light and stood tight-lipped, studying the tracks in the snow. She had a fish in her hand, but now, instead of leaving it on the block, she took it back with her to the house. She didn't intend supplying free handouts to foxes. During the morning she made some attempt at house cleaning, but every few minutes she found herself peering out of the window, or wandering out into the garden, scanning the sky. There was nothing, only the silent grey clouds rolling endlessly down from the north. Once a lone buzzard, prospecting for rabbits in the snow, raised her hopes for a fleeting instant, until she recognised his broad, blunt wings.

In the afternoon it occurred to her that at least she could clear some of the snow from the garden path, and so keep a lookout for the osprey. Despite the cold it was warm work, so much so that after about half an hour she felt the need to shed her jacket. She glanced up towards the fruitcage as she did so, and to her utter astonishment the osprey was there, perched on the roof and watching her as she worked. She had no idea how long he had been there. She had not heard him arrive, but at once she slipped her jacket back on to her shoulders and hurried back to the house to find him a fish.

He was there the next day, and the next. He always arrived at the same time, early in the afternoon, and always he waited until she had laid his fish on the block and retreated down the garden path. Then he would fly down and feed. Afterwards he would sit on the perch in the fruitcage, preen his feathers for a while, and then fall asleep. As soon as he awoke he left, Nicola knew not where.

The long cold spell continued. No more snow fell, but during the long nights frost gripped the earth, and grey clouds, driven by an icy wind, kept the daytime temperature well below freezing. Beneath the frozen snow voles scurried between the frozen stems of the grass, safe from the starving owls that drifted wraithlike over the fields. Rabbits, made desperate with hunger, were driven from their burrows, to strip the bark from young trees. Roe deer stood on their hind legs to reach the few remaining tendrils of ivy that hung from the trees.

Those birds who could rely on a regular supply of food from suburban gardens managed to survive. Others died secretly in the night as they huddled together in a vain attempt to conserve the last vestiges of warmth. The strongest flew south to more congenial climes. Foxes grew thin, and they raided the outskirts of the villages and towns, tipping over the dustbins in search of scraps. Now was their courtship period, and their barking woke the town dogs, who added their clamour to the din, causing lights to appear in bedroom windows as their owners bellowed curses at dogs and foxes alike. Over all the pitiless moon shone white on a sepulchral world, and starlight sparkled on the snow.

February dragged drearily by without any change. Then, in the first week of March, as suddenly and dramatically as the bursting of a dam, the thaw came. It came on a warm west wind, shouting up out of the Atlantic, bearing heavy dark clouds laden with moisture. As the clouds neared the frozen land mass they cooled rapidly. The moisture they carried condensed until it grew too heavy for them to bear, and the wind which bore them tore the burden from their grasp and flung it across the snow-clad hills.

Long afterwards, locals were to shake their heads and declare they had never known its like before. The rain started a little before dusk, and people went to bed rejoicing in the hammering of the gale against their window panes. It was still raining when they woke, and continued all that day and through the next night. It was still coming down on the following morning, though by now the first torrential downpour had eased to a steady rain, filling the gutters and drains, beating against the yielding ramparts of snow that still masked the fields, cutting and tearing and eating away at the white mantle so that it rotted and decayed, breaking into crevices and ravines that ran with water. Trickles became rivulets, rivulets torrents, to unite in a roaring brown flood that swept away all before it. Snow slipped from the sloping fields, sliding downhill and bearing precious topsoil with it, spilling out from the gates and blocking the lanes. Whole hillsides were carried away, trees torn from hedgerows, rocks ripped from their anchorage.

The river raced unchecked down the valley, swirling across fields and roads, bearing the flotsam of centuries – trees, driftwood, fences, barns, with here and there the carcase of a bullock, a sheep, a horse. Bridges were swept away, banks destroyed, new pools created, and beaches of shingle laid where none existed before. Then at last the rain ceased. The wind dropped, patches of blue sky appeared, and somewhere, tremulously, a blackbird began to sing. For the survivors, a new season, of growth, of restoration and hope, had begun.

Thanks to Nicola's ministrations, Iasgair had survived the cold well. He had slept out the thaw, huddled tight against the trunk of the ash tree, out of the driving force of the wind and the rain. His thick mantle of plumage was dense and oil rich, designed by nature to withstand the effects of constant immersion, and it shed the rain just as effectively. Now, though, hunger gnawed at him, driving him from his roost and high into the sky.

He wasted no time on the river, the estuary, or the trout fishery. Instead he flew straight to the one place where he knew he could depend on a meal, the garden where fish was always available without the effort of hunting for it. Nicola, who had missed him during the days of rain, and who had been biting her nails with anxiety in case anything had befallen him, hurried up the garden path with a fish. So the pattern was established, and as day followed day Iasgair the wild fisherman ceased hunting for himself. Instead he became a mendicant, a beggar, content simply to hang around waiting for a handout, entirely dependent on human whim and caprice, until Nicola began to despair of ever being rid of him.

Unknown to Nicola, several times Paul had noticed the osprey hanging about her house and garden as he drove by on his tractor. On the third occasion he guessed the bird was becoming something of a fixture, and he pondered the matter on his way back to the farm. 'Damn bird should be on its way north by now,' he muttered to himself. 'Before it gets too fat to fly.'

By the time be had finished his chores for the day he'd had an idea. 'I think I've solved your problem,' he announced to Mary as they were finishing their tea.

'Which one would that be?' asked Mary suspiciously.

'You know,' said Paul. 'The one you were worrying about at the party, about how to get Martin and Nicola together.'

'They are together,' said Mary. 'I want them in the sack, or in the hay. How are you going to work that one?'

Briefly Paul told her 'Well, don't waste time sitting there drinking tea,' said Mary. 'Get him on the phone.'

Chapter Eleven

'He's become a monster!' Nicola exclaimed. She took the proffered drink but did not taste it. Instead she continued marching up and down.

'Really,' Martin replied, gazing at her over the rim of his glass. His lip twitched, but he was careful to keep the laughter out of his voice. 'Why do you say that?'

'He just sits there, a great lump, a couch potato. Day after day. He's waiting for me every time I put my head out of the door, following me down the garden path, ruling my life. And I swear he's getting more aggressive, more demanding. He nearly took my hat off yesterday, and he's costing me a fortune in fish.'

For a moment Martin did not answer. In fact he knew all about Nicola's problem with the osprey. He knew the answer too. A few days previously he had received a long, rambling telephone call from Paul, ostensibly to enquire how his fish had survived the long cold spell and the ensuing flood. Then he went on to tell Martin that Nicola was being besieged and terrorised by the osprey. 'She's been looking a bit peaky lately,' Paul said. 'Mary and I were wondering if she was still feeling guilty over David's death. His parents blamed her, you know.'

Martin didn't know, and said so. 'Oh yes,' Paul said. 'There was quite a scene at the funeral. Anyway, we were wondering whether a change of scenery would do her good. Mind you, I don't suppose she'd set a foot away from the house as long as that bird is around. Damn thing ought to have gone back to the Highlands of Scotland long ago.'

By now Martin was slightly ahead of Paul. He felt like a fish being played by a somewhat unskilled angler, but under the circumstances he didn't really mind. All the same, he decided to let Paul flounder on a bit. 'I expect one day soon Nicola will wake up and find the osprey gone,' he suggested.

'Fat chance,' replied Paul hastily. 'I reckon someone will have to crate him up and take him there by road. Be nice up there, I imagine, but I can't leave the farm.'

Chuckling to himself, Martin had put down the phone. The thought of a trip up north, with Nicola as his companion, was highly attractive. Visions of Scotland in the spring leapt to mind, of osprey's wheeling high over some windswept loch, of red deer on the hill, and rivers running high with snow melt. Salmon would be running in the clear cold water, leaping the falls and resting in the shadowy depths of the pools. His fishing tackle lay unused in the cupboard. He hadn't had a holiday or a break from the fishery since he bought the place. Suppose he was to offer to take the osprey up north. Suppose he could persuade Nicola to go with him. He might even manage the odd day's salmon fishing.

Now the time had come to propose the plan to Nicola. Suddenly he could think of a dozen reasons why it might not work. After all, the simplest procedure would be to trap the bird, crate it up and send it by rail or air to Inverness, where a representative from the Royal Society For The Protection Of Birds could arrange to meet it, and release the bird into some chosen spot in the wilds. Alternatively, Nicola might want to take the bird herself, without involving him. Or perhaps she would plead indisposition, and refuse to go with him. Come to that, the wretched bird could even take it into its head to fly there, as it was supposed to do. If it didn't drop dead from overfeeding first!

He stood for a moment looking out of the window. After the bitter cold spell the pent up force of spring had exploded in a riot of yellow and gold. Primroses bloomed like pale stars along the margins of the lakes, and the pale green spears of the daffodils flaunted their gold trumpets from the surrounding hills. Blackthorn blossom shone white against the blue of the sky, and over all hung a thin haze of green. 'He ought to be heading north right now,' he murmured, as if thinking out loud. 'Back to Scotland with the rest of his kind.'

'What did you say?' said Nicola. 'I'm sorry. I'm afraid I wasn't listening. I was wondering. Why don't we take him up to Scotland ourselves? Could you afford to take a few days off? I've never seen Scotland in the spring.'

Martin hugged himself with delight. 'I dunno,' he said 'I don't see why not. I've no bookings at the moment, and the fish can take care of themselves.'

'I could get some pictures,' Nicola went on. 'I've got all those shots of the osprey fishing, and pictures of him feeding in the garden in the snow. A set of photos showing his release would round the series off nicely. I've been thinking of writing his story, maybe getting it published. Might even pay for the trip. What do you think?'

'I think it's a great idea. You might even turn a hobby into a career. Where do you suppose we ought to take him?'

'I was wondering about that,' said Nicola. 'The original pair are at a place called Loch Garten, way up in the north, nearly to Inverness, but they won't want him there. He needs to go to a fresh location, somewhere he can find a mate.'

'If "he" is a he,' said Martin.

'He's got that ring on. Maybe we could get in touch with the RSPB and find out more about him. I should have done it sooner, I suppose. Perhaps they could suggest a suitable locality for his new home. Leave it to me. I'll see what I can sort out.'

'We've got to catch him first, remember.'

'Oh that'll be no trouble,' said Nicola airily. 'He always takes a snooze in the fruitcage. We just shut the door on him, and then you go in with your net.'

'Oh aye,' said Martin.

'It'll be easy. He's a pussy cat. Paul had no trouble with him.'

'Hum,' said Martin. Privately he thought that handling a half-starved, half-dead osprey was one thing. Catching up a fit, full fed bird might be a different ball game altogether, but he didn't want to appear cowardly. 'I'd better make a travelling crate.'

'I'm beginning to feel excited,' said Nicola. Impulsively she jumped up and kissed Martin on the cheek. 'There'll still be snow on the mountains. I'd better take plenty of warm clothes.' She reached out for her neglected drink. 'Here's to "operation osprey".'

'Operation osprey', in true Commando fashion, was mounted just after dawn. Nicola crept up the garden path carrying Martin's big landing net, and he followed, staggering slightly under the weight of the crate. Very softly, Nicola closed the door of the fruitcage, and the osprey opened one great yellow eye and glared at her. 'Maybe I should have brought a fish,' she whispered.

'Heavily doped,' said Martin. 'Well, here goes.'

He stepped into the fruitcage, and the osprey, watching his every move, crouched down on the perch and spread its wings. Martin looked at the width of his net and groaned. 'I'll never get him in this,' he muttered.

'Don't loiter,' hissed Nicola. 'Go for him.'

At her words the osprey turned adroitly on the perch and let loose a jet of whitewash which caught Martin square in the midriff. Stepping back, he banged his head on the perch and fell backwards into a patch of virulent young nettles that were flourishing in the nitrogen-rich soil. Unthinking, he put his hands down to push himself up, and got severely stung. Desperately he looked round for help, but Nicola was leaning weakly against the fruitcage, helpless with mirth. The only sound she seemed capable of uttering was a series of small squeaks.

As he struggled to his feet the osprey flapped heavily back up on to the perch, missed its grip, and fell in one corner of the fruitcage. With a snarl of rage Martin discarded his net and seized the bird with his bare hands, pinioning its wings to its body. Triumphantly he bore it across to the crate and bundled it inside before it had time to bring its formidable talons into action.

'Oh, well done!' exclaimed Nicola. 'Now why didn't you do that in the first place, instead of messing about with that silly net?' Then she collapsed into giggles again, while Martin treated her to a withering look before stalking off to the house with as much dignity as he could muster to clean himself up and treat his nettle stings.

An hour later they were on the road, heading north over the flat lands of Somerset. Ahead of them lay over three hundred miles of mostly flat, featureless motorway driving. Not until they reached the fells of north Lancashire would the scenery be in any way inspiring, but they were in good spirits after their flurry of preparation.

Martin drove fast, partly because he did not want the osprey to suffer the ordeal of travel any longer than necessary, and partly because he was already aware of a strong smell drifting from the back of the car, a rank fishy odour which threatened to get worse as the sun poured in through the car windows. He had laboured long into the night making a very superior travelling crate, fitted with a low perch which the osprey stubbornly refused to use, and a sliding tray which he could remove and clean if it became too foul. He had covered the front of the crate with a thick blanket, fortunately an old one, because he had the feeling that once the osprey was safely delivered the only thing to do with the blanket would be to burn it, along with the crate. He wished now he'd thought of installing a couple of air fresheners in the car.

The motorways were relatively free of traffic, and Martin made such good time that by early afternoon they were north of the border. They made a brief stop for lunch, and shortly after another in a lay-by close to a mountain stream. Here Martin was able to wash the tray from the bottom of the crate. Although he managed to relieve it of most of its coating of whitewash he noted to his chagrin that the smell remained, if anything more pungent than ever, despite a thorough scrubbing with sand. Ruefully he pushed it back into place and set off once more, aware that the longer and more tiring part of the journey still lay ahead.

Their destination was not Loch Garten, as they had anticipated, nor anywhere near. Nicola had been in contact with the RSPB, and they in turn had put her in touch with one of their wardens, who told her he had located an ideal site for the osprey's release. He had therefore arranged to meet them and the osprey on an isolated stretch of the road that crossed the bleak watery waste of Rannoch Moor. He would be waiting for them, he told Nicola, and would she please not feed the bird that morning, nor tell anyone of their errand. It all sounded a bit like a scene from a spy story to Nicola, but she had agreed to be at the meeting place soon after dawn.

So they drove on through the afternoon, threading the network of motorways that enmeshed Glasgow like a spider's web, until at last, as the westering sun lit the clouds that crowned the mountain tops, they skirted the shores of Loch Lomond. Still they headed north, past groves of birch trees veiled in a thin mist of green, past dark mountains ribboned with silver streaks as water from the melting snows cascaded down to swell the rivers below. Then, just as dusk was beginning to fall, they rounded a bend in the road and saw a small hotel, set back off the road and nestling in a grove of pine trees. A gravel path curved round through the trees to the door, and the windows were warm orange squares of light in the gathering gloom. The prospect seemed so inviting and alluring that without hesitation Martin swung off the road, even though they were still some twenty miles from their destination.

Nicola, who had been dozing in the passenger seat beside him, came to with a start. 'Where are we?' she murmured.

'I'm not quite sure,' replied Martin, 'but we've nearly reached our rendezvous, and we need somewhere to spend the night. What do you think?'

Nicola yawned and stretched. She ached with the weariness born of the inertia of long distance travel. She needed a bath, a meal and a bed, in that order, and she wasn't too fussy about where. 'If there's a stag's head in the hall, we'll take it,' she replied.

There was a stag's head at the top of the staircase leading up from reception. Better still there was a bright fire burning in the hall, and glasses winked invitingly from a cosy little bar in the corner. They dined on haggis and neaps, partly to celebrate their arrival in Scotland, and partly because the only alternative was grilled gammon and pineapple. They appeared to be the only guests in the hotel.

Afterwards, over a nightcap, Martin broached the delicate subject of his having a few days fishing. Nicola, who had noted the fishing tackle as soon as she had got in the car, and who had been waiting for him to raise the subject, let him flounder around for a while before relenting and putting him out of his misery. Her interest quickened however when he suggested she might take some photographs with a view to an article on the subject. 'I could write it from the woman's angle,' she mused. 'Perhaps get several pieces, even do a humorous one, if you wouldn't mind me making fun.'

Martin relaxed. 'To the non-angler, it's a pretty ridiculous pastime anyway. You'll only be confirming what your readers already suspected.'

Before they turned in for the night they went outside to check on their protégé. There was little they could do for him. Martin had filled a heavy bowl with water and placed it on the floor of the cage, hoping the osprey wouldn't tip it over the back of the car. All seemed quiet, though Martin wondered if they would ever be able to get rid of the smell. Together they tiptoed away, to their separate rooms.

Martin had barely closed his door before he heard a soft tap. Nicola stood outside, hesitant. 'I just wanted to thank you for going to all this trouble. You're a dear.' Then she kissed him, gently, her lips sweet and warm on his, and before he could utter a word she was gone. He fell asleep with the memory of her kiss lingering on his lips.

He woke to grey light, and when he looked out of his window he saw that the world was enveloped in a thick, damp mist. By the time they had breakfasted and settled their bill the fog had thinned. Already shreds of blue sky were showing above the clouds, and the mountain peaks had begun to shrug off their shrouds. The osprey huddled dejectedly on his perch, regarding them with a lacklustre eye, and Martin carefully rearranged the blanket over his crate. 'Not long now, boy,' he murmured. 'And then you'll be free.'

Nicola was silent and subdued as they drove away. The road wound steadily north, crossing small streams where white water foamed between polished black rocks, past small fields littered with boulders, and small plantations of pine trees. Here and there the mist still clung wraithlike to the russet brown slopes of the mountains, where last year's bracken lay like a carelessly flung shawl. Diamond drops clung to the leafless branches of the larch trees, and a chaffinch sang lustily from the topmost branches of a thorn. Ahead the rising sun sparkled on the waters of a distant loch, and a cock pheasant stalked majestically over the dew-drenched grass at the side of the road. Yet the beauty of the morning was lost on Nicola. Already she was mourning the loss of what she had come to regard as her osprey, and she was fully prepared to dislike the warden who was going to tear him from her grasp.

Already she had conjured up a picture of him in her mind: fussy, bumptious, with a bristling beard and anorak, hung with binoculars and cameras, a podgy, garrulous, common little man with a taste for real ale and vulgar tee-shirts. The reality, when they first sighted him framed against a backdrop of rugged granite, was so far removed from her preconceived ideas that she felt herself blush.

He was, she judged, a little over six feet tall, as lean and weatherworn as the ash plant he held in one hand. He was dressed in an old but beautifully cut suit of tweed, his tie neatly knotted, and his brown boots polished to a lustrous shine. At his feet sat an elderly red setter, who regarded them gravely as they got out of the car and walked over to meet his owner.

The man raised his hat as they approached, a gesture which finally won Nicola's heart completely, and introduced himself simply as MacDonald, as though no other title or distinction was necessary. Then he looked rather pointedly at their feet. 'We've a fair drive over the hills, and then a wee walk ahead. I'm thinking it may be a bit moist underfoot.'

Fortunately they had come prepared, and as they donned sweaters and cagoules and put on their boots and gaiters, MacDonald loaded the crate containing the osprey into the back of the Landrover parked nearby. Nicola was carefully assisted into the passenger seat, almost, she thought, stifling a giggle, as though she were a crate of eggs, and Martin was left to shift for himself in the back of the Landrover with the setter, who promptly laid his head in his lap and went to sleep.

There followed one of the most jarring, back-breaking rides of her life, as for over an hour the Landrover, in low gear and four-wheel drive, ground along at near walking pace higher and higher into the hills. Conversation was impossible above the roar of the engine, and in any case MacDonald did not seem given to polite chit-chat. Instead, Nicola contented herself with looking at the scenery, as far as she could while hanging on for dear life.

The track, such as it was, wound endlessly on, skirting bogs and small lochans, the Landrover bouncing over boulders and lurching into hollows as MacDonald fought with the wheel. Once Nicola saw a buzzard, and, to her delight, a small flock of ptarmigan still in their white winter plumage. Once MacDonald shouted something, and looking in the direction he had pointed, she saw a herd of deer bounding away at their approach. Here and there sheep grazed, their long, shaggy fleeces whipped by the wind, but otherwise there was no sign that humans had ever walked this corner of the earth.

At long last the Landrover shuddered to a halt at the edge of a stream, and MacDonald cut the engine. The silence that followed was so profound that Nicola could hear her own breathing. 'We'll walk a bit now, just over the next hill,' said MacDonald. 'Unless, that is, you care to wait in the car.'

Not for worlds was Nicola going to miss seeing the osprey gain his freedom. Swiftly she hopped out of the Landrover and stood breathing the clean cold air of the mountains, looking at the steep slope of scree and rock ahead of them, and wondering how they were going to manage the crate. As if she had spoken out loud MacDonald put her fears at rest. 'We'll not bother with the crate from here on. If you'll just fasten the back of the Landrover behind me, I'll pop our friend into a bag.' So saying, he climbed into the back of the Landrover, and emerged a few moments later with the osprey neatly zipped into a canvas holdall.

Without a word he set off across the stream and up the hill, his staff in one hand and the holdall in the other, the setter following obediently at his heels. He seemed to walk slowly and purposefully, but after about a hundred yards Nicola felt her lungs would burst. Her eyes and nose were streaming, and she was rapidly developing a stitch in her left side. Looking behind her, she saw that Martin did not seem to be in much better shape, but he kept up valiantly, and after a while, to their relief, the ground began to level out somewhat. Just as they thought they could not go another step MacDonald stopped. 'You'll not be used to hill walking, I fancy,' he remarked, studiously avoiding looking at them, as though to witness their distress would be a discourtesy.

Martin grunted. 'I thought Dartmoor could be tough,' he gasped, 'but we've nothing like this.'

MacDonald nodded. 'Aye, most likely you'll have more gentle hills down south,' he murmured apologetically. 'Still, it's not a lot further now.'

They plodded on, skirting black, peat stained pools of water, over thick moss that squelched underfoot, and through low thickets of bog myrtle that grew no higher than their knees, until the ground grew stonier again, and all at once they reached a low saddle between the hills. Ahead of them stretched a vista that made them gasp.

At their feet the ground fell away precipitously, the green mountainside dropping down to a lake set like a jewel in a hollow of the hills. Small waves lapped against a stony shore, and reeds fringed the far margins. In the centre of the loch stood a little island, on which grew a modest clump of pine trees. 'A small shred of the ancient forest of Caledonia,' murmured MacDonald, and with a start Martin realised he was referring to the trees. 'Aye,' said MacDonald. 'Once those trees grew across the length and breadth of the Highlands, but our forebears cut them down, partly for fuel, partly because they were a hiding place for wolves, robbers and bears. It was a great loss, for we'll never see the like again.' He stood for a moment lost in thought, and then added, 'Still, it'll be a grand place for our friend here to pass the summer don't you think?'

He turned to Nicola. 'No doubt it's yourself who will wish to set the captive free?'

Nicola shook her head, unslinging her camera from around her neck. Understanding, MacDonald put the holdall on the ground, bent down and slid back the zip. The head of the osprey appeared, but he made no attempt to leave the bag. Instead he crouched there, his yellow eyes surveying the landscape. Then suddenly he gave a mighty heave, flung himself clear of the confines of his prison and flopped clumsily across the ground. Next moment he was airborne, climbing with rapid wing beats high into the sky above them. He circled round, once, twice, and as Nicola clicked away with her camera he spread his wings and glided down towards the lake. As he neared the waters of the loch he soared again, and then dropped down into the crown of one of the trees on the island. There he settled to preen himself. Nicola watched until the bird, the loch and the island were no more than a vague blur, and as she turned away she knew from the lump in her throat that it was not just the wind that made her eyes water.

Chapter Twelve

They were back at the road, making their farewells to Mac-Donald, when he spied the fishing rods in the car. 'I see you are planning to try the fishing,' he said. 'Is it the salmon you are interested in?'

Martin nodded. 'We thought we'd head over to the Spey, see where the osprey first nested, and maybe have a day on the water.'

MacDonald thought for a while. 'I have a cousin owns a short stretch. I'm sure he'll make you welcome for a day. There are three good holding pools.' He produced a small notebook and pencil. 'I'll write down his telephone number for you to ring, and I'll phone him myself tonight to tell him to expect you.'

When Martin tried to stammer his thanks MacDonald waved them away. 'Ach, Dougal's a great one for the birds. I'm sure he'd be pleased to help anyone who has gone to as much trouble as you have. Enjoy your day, and good luck.'

They drove north east, along the shores of Loch Tay and the river of the same name, and the journey took a lot longer than they expected. The sun shone from a clear blue sky, the mountain peaks wore a frosting of snow, and the waters of the loch sparkled in the spring sunshine, so that Nicola was forever wanting to stop and take pictures, and Martin gazed longingly at the foaming waters of the river, eager to catch just a glimpse of a leaping salmon. What with one thing and another the day was almost spent before they drew near their destination, and Martin began watching for somewhere to spend the night, for he knew that in Scotland the evening meal was served early, and if they were not careful they would go supperless to bed.

So it was with some relief that he saw a sign advertising an hotel a few hundred yards further along the road. The exterior of the premises, as they drew closer, did not look half so inviting as the place they had found the previous evening, but they were tired and hungry and so they stopped, just to take a look. It was fortunate that they did, for once inside they received an extremely pleasant surprise.

They had happened by chance on an establishment which, rather than set out to cater for the passing tourist trade, relied almost entirely on regular visitors, who came at the same time each year, mainly for the fishing, and who had over the years become old friends. As it happened, there were two rooms vacant, so Martin and Nicola were welcomed to stay, and they soon found it was rather like joining a private house party.

Once again they had adjoining rooms, tucked away up in the top storey of the hotel. There was a door set in one wall of Martin's room, and, thinking it was a closet, he tried to open it. It proved to be locked, and he had just turned away when it opened and Nicola poked her head round it.

For a moment they stood there looking at each other, neither one wishing to speak. Then next moment she was in his arms, her body moulded to his and her lips returning his kisses with an ardour that made his head spin and his heart hammer at his side. Trembling, he tried to draw her down on the bed, but she pushed him away and covered his lips with her hand. 'Not yet,' she whispered. 'I'm more compliant when I'm fed. I'll see you in the bar.' Then she was gone, and Martin heard the bolt click shut on the door, leaving him shaking his head in bewilderment and rapture on the other side.

The bar was open, and business was brisk, though no bartender was in attendance. Instead each guest helped himself from the array of bottles, making a note of what he had taken in a record book provided for the purpose. Whisky, not surprisingly, seemed to be the preferred drink, and there was a wide selection of single malts from which to choose. Martin was nursing a large measure of Talisker when Nicola

113

appeared. The sight of her brought him to his feet, his jaw dropping in admiration and surprise. Once again Nicola had wrought one of her transformations. She was dressed in a simple high-necked frock of jade green silk, dark stockings, and silver sandals. For jewellery she wore a single heavy gold chain. She looked exquisite, and Martin told her so. She grinned wickedly. 'I'm a bit overdressed for these Edinburgh housewives, but I felt like a change.' She looked hard at his glass. 'Are you going to get me one of those?'

Since it was Sunday, a fact they had both forgotten, dinner took the form of a cold buffet, but one glimpse of the groaning sideboard assured them they would not go hungry. For starters there was a choice of soup, venison pâté, scotch eggs or melon. To follow, they could chose from a side of beef, a whole salmon, chicken, cold ham, and ox tongue. An assortment of pastries, fruit, biscuits and cheese and celery completed the display. The guests helped themselves to whatever they fancied, while trimly dressed waitresses stood to one side, ready to whisk plates away as soon as they were emptied.

Ravenous after their long day, they ate hugely, and afterwards sat in the hotel lounge nursing a small nightcap, saying little, content to enjoy each other's company. To Martin's relief, most of the other guests also seemed eager to retire early, so their disappearance was unlikely to cause comment. He stood by the window in his darkened bedroom, looking out across a stretch of parkland to where moonlight shimmered on the waters of a small loch. Somewhere a great northern diver called, and as if in answer an owl answered from a nearby clump of pines. Then he heard the soft click of the door.

Several times in the night he woke to feel the nearness of her, and instantly he was yet again roused by her touch, her smell, the soft roundness of her body close to his. He felt like a boy, eager, inept, fumbling, yet when he attempted to apologise she laughed, a throaty chuckle. 'Am I complaining?' she whispered, and drew him to her yet again.

They breakfasted on porridge served with sugar and cream, brown trout freshly grilled, bacon and eggs, and white toast with fresh butter and Dundee marmalade, all washed down with several cups of coffee. Afterwards, so replete they both felt they wouldn't need to eat again for at least another week, they set off to explore the surrounding countryside. First they visited the RSPB centre at Loch Garten, where the original nest site stood under constant twenty-four hour guard. It was, they both agreed, an astonishing feat of organisation.

The nest was built on the very top of an old dead pine tree, in the middle of a clearing in the forest, and securely fenced against intruders. Instead, spectators had access to a range of wooden buildings hidden discreetly among the trees, and incorporating a shop, and what could only be described as a viewing lounge, since the room was well lit and spacious, with even carpet on the floor. Binoculars were provided, giving a view of the nest site through observation slits, and close circuit television gave a constant close-view of the hen bird perched on the vast, unwieldy pile of sticks that formed the nest. Unfortunately they had timed their visit too early in the year to witness much activity, indeed the warden informed them that the pair had just arrived. Apart from some desultory attempts to repair the nest, nothing was happening.

They lingered on for about half an hour, until a coach party arrived. Judging by the accents, Nicola guessed they came from somewhere in the Midlands. Most of the visitors were well past middle age, the women immaculately coiffured and dressed, the men redolent of aftershave. After a glance at the osprey, most of the newcomers turned to browse among the souvenirs. An air of boredom and lassitude hung over the group, and after a few moments, by tacit consent, Nicola and Martin made their escape into the sunshine. 'I've watched a lot of animals and birds,' Martin remarked, 'but never in such a fragrant atmosphere.'

They wandered off down the forest track that led towards the car park and the road. Through the trees they caught a glimpse of water and next moment they stood on the rocky shore of a small, tree lined loch. For the rest of that long golden day, as the sun shone and the chaffinches called from the birch trees, they explored the loch's margins, following twisty paths through the pines which every now and then thinned to give them a fresh perspective – a bracken cloaked

115

mountainside; a reedy bay, mirror calm, where water birds rode at rest; a granite outcrop framed against the azure sky. The fragrance of the pines mingled with bog myrtle, and the sharp, sweet-sour smell of the water filled their nostrils. They lay down to rest beneath the massive bole of an ancient Scots pine, and Martin wanted to make love there and then, but Nicola, laughing, fought him off. 'I'm not combing pine needles out of my hair for the rest of the day. Be patient, and wait until tonight.'

Dinner, on that second night in the hotel, was even better than the first time. Afterwards Martin telephoned the contact MacDonald had given him about the fishing. Evidently this Dougal was impressed by what his cousin had told him, because he not only invited Martin to enjoy a day on his water, but promised to send his keeper to collect him, and to show him the best salmon lies. So it was in a state of high elation that Martin returned to report to Nicola, who was waiting patiently in the hotel lounge.

They were ready and waiting when the Range Rover pulled into the hotel car park early the next morning. Martin had expected the keeper to be a grizzled, taciturn highlander, but the man behind the wheel turned out to be in his early twenties, slim, fair-haired and English. 'I'm Michael,' he announced, as he helped Martin transfer his fishing gear from the car. 'The guv'nor sends his regrets, but he's unable to meet you this morning. He might be able to join you by the river this afternoon, so if you see a decrepit old poacher type wandering along, it'll be him.' He let the vision hang in the air, somehow managing to imply affection rather than disrespect. 'You'll be anxious to get at the fishing no doubt,' he remarked as he let in the clutch. 'It's a bit overbright, but there's still plenty of snow water coming off the hills, and there are a few fish in the pools.'

They pulled into a lay-by near the bridge. Below them the river sparkled in the sunlight, a long rippling run that ended in a deep pool, rocky and tree fringed. Michael leaned on the parapet of the bridge. 'Yon's the first pool. Fish it slowly and carefully. The fish may be anywhere. If you get an offer but miss him, leave him and try again later in the day. Come on, I'll show you the other two.'

116

The two men set off downstream. Nicola sat on the bridge, content for the moment to bask in the morning sunlight, and watched them go. Something about their manner, their total absorption in themselves and the river, reminded her of two small boys let out to play, so that for a moment she felt a wave of almost maternal love and affection for them both.

She was alone with the sounds of the morning – the faint sigh of the wind in the pines, the musical murmur of the water as it rippled over the stones, the song of a chaffinch in a nearby birch tree – and she found herself speculating on the depth of her feeling for Martin. It wasn't love of the breathless, heart rending sort that put you off your food and kept you waiting near the telephone lest it should ring, longing to hear his voice at the other end. It was rather a snug feeling of warmth and security and comfort, of easy comradeship and relaxed good humour. It wasn't the sort that kept you awake at nights, or rather, she thought, with a small, self-satisfied smirk, it wasn't the sort that kept you awake at nights in an agony of desire.

Was it sufficient? She wasn't sure, but it was enough to be getting on with. Martin had proved a most satisfactory lover, eager and anxious to please, yet with a boyish, refreshing delight in exploring her body, taking his own pleasure and enchanting her in the process. He had stamina too, she reflected rather ruefully, easing her aching back.

She heard a clatter among the stones, and looking up she saw the two men returning along the river bank. When Martin saw her he waved and grinned, raising both his thumbs before going to the Landrover to unload his tackle. Nicola watched from the bridge as he went through the ritual of donning chest waders, fishing waistcoat and hat, before assembling his rod and threading the heavy fly line through the rings. Michael lingered at his side, poring over the contents of a fat aluminium fly box.

He grunted with approval as he prodded the exotic confections of fur and feather, peacock herl and buck tail, squirrel tail and jay's wing, tinsel and wire of silver and gold. Finally he picked out the one of his choice. It was a small tube, less than two inches long, with a silver body and a cape of shining black squirrel tail, with two eyes fashioned from the tiny feathers from the cape of a jungle cock. 'This one,' he announced, 'and if it doesn't do the trick try one a size smaller.'

Martin threaded the silver stoat on to his leader, and tied a new treble hook on the point. Then he set the lure firmly against the shank of the treble.

Meantime Michael had taken a hamper from the Landrover and set it down under the bridge. 'Lunch,' he announced. 'When you are ready. I'll leave you to it. Good luck.' Then he was gone, and Martin and Nicola stood looking at each other as the growl of the diesel engine died away in the distance. All Nicola could think of was, 'Why the hat?' He never wore a hat, because he said he'd worn one too long during his time in the marines.

'Safety precaution,' said Martin, in answer to her query. 'This little chap,' and he indicated the tube fly hitched to his rod, 'is tied on a brass tube, to give it enough weight to sink. When I'm casting, it's flying through the air at about sixty miles an hour. If it hit me on the head it could knock me cold. Besides, I'd look a right wally with a treble hook stuck in my head.'

Secretly Nicola thought he looked ridiculous anyway, a sort of cross between a Samurai warrior and a Michelin man. It was the waistcoat that did it, she decided. It bristled with pockets and zips and gadgets, the purpose of which she could only guess at. 'Like the waistcoat,' she said.

'It's got sixteen pockets,' said Martin proudly, 'including a big one at the back.'

He was a boy, thought Nicola. At least where fishing was concerned. And yet he seemed so mature in every other way. Perhaps all men were boys at heart, and maybe it was better that they should so compartmentalise their lives, than be childish all the time. Perhaps that had been the trouble with David, that he had been completely grown up, that he had lost the ability to play. Suddenly the cliché, 'young at heart' took on a new and profound meaning.

'Well!' said Martin. 'Better get started.' He set off down to the river, not looking back, expecting her to follow. She picked up her camera and followed him, not quite knowing what was expected of her, somehow sensing he was not going

118

to explain. He waded out into the water until it was just above his knees, and began to cast.

Seen thus, the rod like a live thing in his hands, framed in the arch of the bridge, he looked less ridiculous. The whole made a pleasing picture, and the light was right, so she got busy with her camera. He worked down the pool a step at a time, the line curving out in a graceful arc which sent the small fly down and across the current, every action rhythmical, balletic, almost hypnotic to watch. After about half an hour, though, Nicola began to get bored. As a spectator sport, salmon fishing seemed to lack a certain something. Nothing was happening. Martin seemed utterly engrossed with his casting, and a faint but icy breeze had arisen, making her shiver despite her layers of warm clothing. She decided to explore a little further down the river.

A shout from Martin made her stop and turn, thinking he had hooked a fish. 'Don't go downstream,' he called. 'You might disturb the fish.'

Obediently Nicola sat down, but she felt a faint stir of resentment. After another ten minutes Martin reeled in his line and waded ashore. 'Sorry,' he said, 'but if you spook a fish close in to the bank it's apt to take off and panic other fish in the pool. Then it'd be half an hour before they settle down again. Come on. We'll try the next pool. And if you want to stretch your legs keep well away from the water.'

It had been a long time since anyone had given Nicola a direct order forbidding her from doing something. The thought came into her head unbidden: anyone would think we were married, the way he's behaving. Immediately she realised she was being childish, and sternly she tried to dismiss the notion. It was Martin's day. He had looked forward to it, earned it, and being churlish was no way to repay him for all he had done for her. She was here to take photographs, in the unlikely event of his catching a fish, and her personal feelings did not count.

About fifty yards downstream the river curved in a right-hand bend, the white water foaming between limestone rocks until it met a barrier formed of harder rock. Here its pace was slowed, and the current fell swirling and tumbling into a deep pool. They stood on a stony shingle shore which fell precipitously away into deep water. Most of the pool was in bright sunlight, but beneath the far bank it was in shade.

The fish lay in deep water about halfway down the pool. Two nights ago she had left the sea on the high tide, in company with two smaller fish, and entered the long arm of the estuary that wound down to the coast. Throughout that night and most of the next day she and her companions had forged swiftly and steadily upstream, entering this particular pool just before dawn. Now they rested in mid-water, hugging the sheer rock face of the cliff, exerting just enough energy to hold against the current, the two smaller fish slightly below and beneath her.

Martin stood on a flat rock near the head of the pool and scowled at the water. 'Sooner fish this with a worm than a fly,' he grumbled. 'Still, here goes.' He dropped the fly in the water and began to shake out line. Lower down the pool, and standing well back from the water, Nicola focused her camera on him and watched through the viewfinder as he started to cast.

The big fish was wakeful, irritable, ill at ease. There was a patch of sea lice clustered by her tail, feeding from her bloodstream. She had tried to shake them, rubbing herself against the rocks, once leaping high out of the water. Still the lice clung obstinately to her scales. Now, as Martin's lure swam slowly towards her, flickering and winking in the clear water high above her, she felt the sea lice again and took off in a slow circle round the pool. The other fish followed her, and by the time they had returned to their station Martin was preparing for yet another cast.

This time he aimed to cast more at right angles to the flow, so that the fly fell a little higher upstream, and by the time the lure reached the fish it had sunk deeper. Now it swam slowly, tantalisingly across her vision, pulsing, throbbing as the current gently fanned the gleaming black hair, the silver body sending little winks and darts of light. In sudden rage she surged forward and struck at it, sucking it in on a great gulp of water and crushing it against the roof of her mouth.

Satisfied that she had destroyed the source of her irritation, she tried to eject it, but as she turned to regain the sanctuary of her lie one point of the treble hook sank into her lower

120

jaw, just at the angle of her mouth. She felt a sudden sideways strain as an unknown force pulled her head round. Angered again, she shook her head in an effort to be rid of it. On the shore opposite Martin gave a great shout as he felt the sudden weight on his rod, and the unmistakable stubborn slow shaking that signalled a fish.

The salmon withstood the pressure for a few moments more, but the pull forced her head round, bringing her body broadside to the current, and try as she might she could not remain head on to the current. Suddenly alarmed, she channelled all her power into one mighty thrust of her tail, which swung her round and carried her off downstream in a long, upward slanting run towards the shallow water at the tail of the pool. There she broke surface, leaping high into the clear sunlit air.

The sudden eruption startled Nicola so much that had the camera not been slung around her neck she would have dropped it. She could only stand, gaping, as the surface of the pool subsided and Martin ran towards her down the shore, frantically trying to regain the line the fish had stripped off his reel. She could feel her heart hammering and her knees shaking as she watched the rod bucking and jerking, the line hissing through the water.

Then the fish surfaced again, shaking its head in fury or pain, she couldn't decide which, as it tried to free itself from the hook. Martin was at once laughing and swearing, now backing up the shore, now running back towards the water's edge, as the fish sounded deep and sped off to the head of the pool. Nicola had by now completely forgotten about her camera.

At last the fish was beginning to tire. It made one more fast run down the pool, but this time Martin was able to stop it and turn it, and by clamping down on the reel with one hand he was able to walk the fish back up the pool to a little bay where he hoped he could land it. Here the fish contented itself with cruising round in slow circles, weakening all the time, but not yet ready to submit. Nicola had recovered sufficiently to take a couple more pictures of Martin playing the fish. Then she moved closer and looked down into the water.

For the first time she saw the salmon clearly, a great gleaming bar of silver twisting and writhing in the jade-green water of the pool. She saw the size of it, and the sensuous grace of its streamlined curving body, but it was the expression on the face that made her go cold and gasp in horror. The eye, with its dark pupil and golden iris, stared back at her. The great gill slit flared like a wound. The mouth was open wide in what appeared to be a silent scream of agony. 'Let it go!' she pleaded. 'Oh! Please. Let it go.'

For a moment Martin looked at her in stunned disbelief. Then he laughed. 'Not likely,' he said. 'Not at this stage.'

Then she could only watch, as the salmon's struggles grew weaker and the circles grew smaller, until at last the great fish turned over on its side. At that moment Nicola looked away, so she did not see Martin reach down and grasp the fish by its tail. Nor did she see him club the fish on the head, but she heard the blows, and the rattle of the tail on the shingle as the salmon died. Suddenly Nicola knew that she was faced with a choice. She could express her true feelings and thereby risk spoiling Martin's moment of triumph, and perhaps lose his friendship, or she could hide them, and live with her conscience.

Her mind was made up. Turning, she looked down at Martin, bent on one knee over the fish. 'It's a beauty,' she exclaimed. 'I bet you're pleased.'

'Beyond belief,' said Martin. 'Fifteen pounds if she's an ounce, and absolutely sea fresh! He held out both hands, palm downwards. 'I expect I'll stop trembling after a while.'

He took a salmon bass out of the pocket in the back of his waistcoat and tenderly laid the fish in it. 'I wonder why,' he murmured, 'when out at sea and on the estuary, men haul fish out in nets like so many sacks of coal, do I feel remorse at killing one fish?'

Nicola said nothing. He turned and washed his hands at the water's edge. 'I think a break for lunch is indicated, don't you? Let's go and see what goodies Dougal has packed for us.' They set off back to the bridge, Martin carrying the salmon, Nicola trailing slightly behind. If Martin had noticed her failure to take any more pictures, he made no comment.

It was a simple meal, but substantial. There was a game

pie, crusty rolls and butter, cheese and fruit, and there was a quarter bottle of whisky, a smoky single malt, and not one but two bottles of claret. Martin peered at the label. 'The man keeps a good cellar for a Scot,' he muttered. 'If we see this lot off we're both liable to fall in the river.'

Nicola did not feel hungry, but the warmth of the malt soothed her, and with the sight and smell of the pie when it was cut open her appetite returned. They munched in silence for a while, listening to the music of the river. 'You weren't very happy back there for a while,' said Martin suddenly.

It was at once a statement and a question. Caught unawares, although in truth she had been analysing her thoughts before he spoke, Nicola was unable to hide her true feelings. 'I'm sorry,' she said, 'but although reason tells me you were perfectly justified in catching that fish, my heart tells me it was suffering needlessly, and that you were the cause of its pain.'

Martin was silent for a long while. I've done it now, thought Nicola miserably. Me and my big mouth. Aloud she said, 'I should never have come. I should have left you to enjoy yourself, without me putting a damper on things.'

Martin took a swig of wine. 'It's a cruel world out there, lady,' he said gently. 'You can either face up to it, or hide away. With luck you'll die not knowing a tenth of it. But it's there, and it won't go away.' He waited for Nicola to defend herself, but she made no reply, so he went on. 'I don't have to excuse my behaviour.' He was about to add: to you nor anyone else, but he decided to keep the debate impersonal. 'To be absolutely honest, I don't know whether that fish back there was suffering pain, as we understand it, whether it was terrified, or whether it was just plain furious. I do know I take no pleasure from the thought of inflicting pain. If I did, if I was in any way a sadist, then folk would have grounds to pity and despise me. Sure there are plenty of sadists out there, supermarket managers, prison warders, overbearing fathers, army officers, school teachers. Aye, and women too, who enjoy tormenting and humiliating and dominating humans and animals alike.

'Only I'm not one of them. If you ask me why hunting and fishing means so much to me, then the simple answer is that

123

I don't know. I do know that I am anxious to minimise any suffering I may cause by despatching the fish as quickly and humanely as possible. I also know that the instinct to hunt and kill is an old madness, one that drove man out of the warmth and comfort of his shelter in the cold of the paleolithic dawn to hunt the musk ox and the woolly mammoth. And it's an instinct that has served him well, through ten thousand years of living in the wilderness, before the dawn of what we laughingly call civilization. And it's part of me. I could give up fishing tomorrow and I'd come to no harm, but part of my life would be missing, and it's important to me. I'm not prepared to renounce my heritage, or insult the integrity of my forefathers.'

Abruptly he got to his feet. 'I'm wasting time. There's another pool to fish, and I want to give it a try before Michael comes to collect us. You can follow me down if you like.'

Then he was gone, leaving Nicola sitting beside the bridge. She felt at once guilty and resentful, though in all honesty she felt she had done nothing wrong. She was utterly miserable at the thought of hurting Martin, but she knew that it would be a long time before she could rid herself of the image of the salmon, with its eyes staring and its mouth open wide, battling for existence in the jade waters of the pool.

Chapter Thirteen

Heat and light flooded the glen, crisping the dried lichen that clung to the rock and baking the parched earth where deer had torn the scant vegetation from its brief hold on existence. A lizard flickered across the stone, a swift scribble of life that vanished almost immediately beneath a clump of heather. Summer had come to the Highlands, as it had done ten thousand times before, since the last of the great glaciers had melted, freeing the land from its icy tomb and surrendering it once more to warmth and life. Since the Arctic Ocean lay not far to the north, and since the ice age was still but a recent event in the geological time scale, the summers were no more than fleeting interludes between long winters of darkness and cold. Yet occasionally, as now, the sun blazed down, bleaching the azure blue of the sky, setting the hills to shimmer in the heat, and quickening the pace of life, fortifying the natural world against the winter to come.

The history of the landscape was written in the stone. From his perch high in the pine tree Iasgair saw it all: the rock pavements laid bare by the slow progress of the ice; the marks of its passage engraved in the stone; the raised beaches caused by the uplifting of land relieved of its burden of ice; the depressions that remain forever waterlogged. One such hollow formed the loch he now surveyed, a shallow, sunlit bowl full of clear mineral-rich water that drained from the surrounding hills.

The pine tree which Iasgair had selected as his roost was the tallest, and oldest, of the group which flourished on the small island in the middle of the loch. This particular tree was now past its prime, and though it still put forth new needles every spring, and still bore a crop of cones each autumn, several of its major branches were dead, devoid of needles and bark, so that they shone silvery white in the sun. Over the years they had seasoned and hardened, so that although they creaked and groaned in every squall that blew down off the mountains, they were as safe and secure as the living limbs.

The island on the loch was too small for habitation. Fire could not reach it there, and new growth was safe from the nibbling teeth of sheep, deer and hare. The timber it might supply was not worth the cost of cutting and transporting across the loch. The trees survived, and their roots embraced the unmarked graves of three cottagers buried there centuries ago by relatives who wished to protect their corpses from the wolves. The dead became the island's guardians, for no highlander would disturb their slumbers by any profane or sacrilegious act.

Full fed, Iasgair drowsed on his perch, soaking in the warmth, rousing himself now and again to mark the concentric rings on the surface of the loch, caused by rising trout. Viewed from above, the loch resembled a giant lens, and indeed it was a focal point for many forms of life. A wigeon led her flotilla of young through a forest of reeds, carefully skirting the place where a pair of little grebes patrolled the territory surrounding their floating nest. In the shallow water by the shore a heron stood, statuesque, its unblinking eye fixed on the frogs that sported in the deeper water among the lily pads.

Beneath the surface of the loch life teemed, in a density ten times that which populated the surrounding hills. There were other fish besides the trout – pike, perch and eels – all of which preyed upon the abundant insect life, and sometimes on each other. Plant life flourished in the warm sunlit waters, and in their green shade newts danced in ritual courtship, the female catching each individual egg as she laid it, and attaching it to a leaf.

All around them the larger insects foraged for food, hatched, mated and died. A dragonfly larva climbed up a reed stem, emerging into the sunlight to await its metamorphosis into a winged insect. Shrimps scudded over the sand, combing the detritus for food; water beetles whirled in an iridescent dervish dance on the surface film.

Yet by far the greatest volume of life, both in numbers and weight, belonged to the chironomid larva. Their populations were now at their peak, and already they were turning into the curse of Scotland, the biting midge. Though the fish and the larger insects gorged on them every hour of the day, still vast numbers survived to reach maturity. They were small, feeble, ineffectual fliers, so weak that the merest puff of wind, the smallest shower of rain, would render them helpless. Yet when the air was calm and warm their attacks were so persistent and frenzied that they maddened every living thing.

Even the lordly red deer were not immune. At this time of year the stags were in velvet, and their antlers were soft and suffused with blood. When they came to drink at the loch side the midges descended in clouds, swarming over the thin sensitive skin that covered the antlers, seeking the most vulnerable spots at which to press home their attack. So as soon as the deer had drunk their fill they departed, back up on to the high peaks, where they were sure of finding a breeze to drive their attackers away. Yet even so they suffered, the midges at times drawing up to a pint of blood a week from each individual deer. Sooner or later the blood sucking midges died, or were caught and eaten by other insects or birds. So, drop by minuscule drop, the minerals dissolved in the blood of the deer, and those harvested by the midges from the bottom of the loch, were recycled and returned to the high hills, to replenish the soil and nourish the plant life there.

Iasgair too suffered from the attention of the biting clouds of midges, but less often, for there was usually some circulation of air around his lofty perch. At times though they roused him from his full fed torpor, sending him spiralling into the sky above the loch, there to ride a thermal of warm air and soar above the hills. Occasionally another osprey, always a young, immature bird like himself, would spy him from afar and join him briefly in his aerial flight, but always, respecting his territorial rights, would leave him without trespassing near the loch.

The short summer drifted imperceptibly towards its climax. The long days of June, in which the sun scarcely set, seemingly condemned to circle the earth in endless orbit, began to shrink, as night gained ascendancy. MacDonald visited the loch frequently, making the long journey over the mountains from the road just to satisfy himself that the osprey had come to no harm. Since he was not a man to waste an opportunity, he carried with him a light trout rod and a few casts of flies, and usually spent an hour or two fishing in the loch. He never kept more than a brace of fish, and often departed empty-handed, having rejected all the trout he caught as undersized.

In no way did he ever feel he was depriving the osprey of its precious food supply. He had been familiar with the loch since his boyhood, and knew that it carried a stock of fish more than adequate to feed a whole family of ospreys, in addition to his needs. No other angler, to his knowledge, made the arduous journey over the hills to fish the loch, for there was plenty of good fishing easier of access. This isolation, and the wealth of its food supply, was why he had chosen the site as a suitable locality for a breeding pair of the great fish hawks.

He didn't see the osprey on every occasion, but he noted its presence often enough to know that it had established itself in the vicinity, and guessed it was only a question of time before it attracted a mate, maybe as early as the following year. Accordingly, one day in late summer, he wrote to Nicola informing her that the osprey had settled down and was flourishing in its new home.

Nicola received the news with mixed feelings. On the one hand she was relieved to learn that the osprey had survived in its new home. On the other she had no great wish to be reminded of an interlude in which she had come close, if indeed she had not actually succeeded, to making a complete fool of herself.

She had spent the rest of that fateful day sitting alone by the river, brooding on the insensitivity of man. She was honest enough to admit to herself that it was Martin's attitude to her, as much as the suffering caused to the fish, that rankled. He had treated her with scant courtesy through-

128

out the day, and utterly refused to agree to a plea which, although it may have been unreasonable, had been uttered from the heart. This at a time when she would have thought that Martin's whole existence would have been attuned towards her happiness. So be it. It was as well she had discovered his true nature before committing herself entirely.

She had sat waiting, hoping that Martin would seek her out to apologise and beg forgiveness, but when he returned, fishless, his attitude was friendly but cool. The romance that had flowered so briefly withered and blackened like a dahlia in the frost, and that night they had slept in separate rooms. The drive back was accomplished mostly in silence, as each waited for the other to make the first attempts at reconciliation.

Since then they had seen little of each other. They had met on a couple of occasions, and Martin had phoned her several times, suggesting an outing, but each time she had put him off, pleading a previous engagement. In fact, over the weeks she had grown increasingly antisocial, instead devoting all her energies towards the long neglected garden, working until she was aching with fatigue, and steadily growing browner, slimmer and fitter.

Even Paul and Mary saw little of her. When Mary, with her usual directness, had asked Nicola how the affair was progressing Nicola had merely sniffed. 'If he wants a doormat he knows where he can buy one. He's not going to wipe his feet all over me.'

But she wouldn't enlighten Mary any further. Martin was equally reticent. 'She want's a poodle, not a man,' was his only comment. So there the matter rested. Both Paul and Mary were baffled, but beyond agreeing that both Martin and Nicola were behaving like spoiled children, they could do nothing to help.

Nicola could see no reason why she should inform Martin about the osprey's welfare. She wrote a short note to MacDonald, thanking him for his news and saying she would be pleased to hear if the bird ever returned to the loch and found a mate. Then she went back out into the garden.

August slipped away. September brought a succession of

warm, cloudless days, when the sun sucked the moisture from the earth, returning it in the form of dew as the temperature fell each night. Mushrooms glowed white in the short, sheep-bitten pasture of the meadows, and blackberries glistened in the hedge ...s. Far to the north, in the high mountains, the nights brought the first frosts, staining the bracken fern rust red and gilding the leaves of the birch trees.

The stranger came to the loch one morning, when thin cat ice crackled at the shore, and the sere reeds were white with hoarfrost. Like Iasgair, the cormorant was a fisherman, but unlike the ospreys, he fished under water. His plumage was blackish with a green gloss, except for white patches on his chin and thighs, and he was armed with a large yellow beak, cruelly hooked at the tip. He had hatched from a pale blue egg laid in a mound of dried seaweed and sticks on a cliff face overlooking the sea, but he was equally at home in sea water or in fresh. He was a large bird, but squat, almost reptilian in appearance, like some throwback to the age of dinosaurs.

He hunted his prey by pursuing it under water, propelled by powerful strokes of his webbed feet, his wings folded tight against his flanks. From time to time he was forced to return to shore or seek the sanctuary of a convenient rock in order to dry his plumage, for he lacked any means of waterproofing his feathers. His appetite was as gross as his appearance, and he consumed his own weight of fish in a day.

Iasgair took exception to the cormorant from the moment of its arrival, most probably because he perceived it as a competitor for his food supply. Hitherto the other fish-eating birds had posed no threat. The heron kept to the margins. The kingfisher was too small to be significant. The others – the goosander, the red-breasted merganser, the tufted ducks and the terns – all took fish, but of such small size as to be of no interest to the osprey.

The cormorant took more substantial prey, fish of half a pound and more. Worse, its continual voyaging to and fro under the surface of the loch disturbed many more fish than were caught. Trout loved to lie just below the surface, basking in the sunlit shallows, or rising to suck in some insect struggling on the surface. The cormorant unsettled them, driving them into deeper water where they lay skulking among the mud and stones at the bottom of the loch, fearful and ready to flee at the slightest shadow.

These tactics did not save them from the cormorant, who singled out his victims, pursuing them relentlessly until an error of judgement, or sheer fatigue, put them in range of his beak. They did, however, become inaccessible to Iasgair, who relied on ambushing an unsuspecting victim as it lay just below the surface. Perhaps he knew the cormorant was to blame for his failures. Perhaps he simply used the other bird as a target on which to vent his anger, but he took to attacking the cormorant every time it surfaced, driving it back under water.

These tactics did not deter the cormorant from his purpose. Indeed it is doubtful whether he was ever at all inconvenienced by them. He swallowed his prey under water and came to the surface only to breathe. By the time Iasgair launched his attack he was ready to dive again, and since, strangely, Iasgair did not pursue the cormorant once he was out of the water, the cormorant was able to rest and dry his plumage in peace.

Two days passed, and Iasgair grew more and more incensed at the presence of the cormorant on the loch, launching himself from his perch at the top of the pine tree and flying low over the loch, just in time to see his enemy disappear below the surface. Sometimes he would hover above the water at the spot where the cormorant had dived, only to find that his tormentor had reappeared somewhere else. So the game of tag went on, and the cormorant grew careless, not bothering to dive until the last moment. It was a mistake that was to prove fatal.

Hunger drove Iasgair away from the loch to hunt further afield, and so he was absent for long periods, during which time the cormorant grew more negligent than before. Yet Iasgair always returned to his favourite roost in the old pine, and one morning he woke to the realisation that his old enemy was nowhere to be seen.

The sun was just rising. Tendrils of mist curled off the cold waters of the loch, and the surface shimmered and flashed with pinpoints of light. Iasgair lofted off his branch and planed low across the water, prospecting for an early trout. He glimpsed a vague shape below him moving slowly through the water, hovered for an instant, and then closed his wings and dived.

He struck the cormorant high on the back, just behind the shoulders, and the weight of his strike thrust the bird deeper into the water. His talons sank deep, through skin and muscle and into bone, and pain drove the cormorant to dive deeper, kicking out with his powerful webbed feet in an endeavour to escape his tormentor. All he succeeded in doing was to drag Iasgair after him.

Iasgair oared the water frantically with his wings, sinking deeper with every moment that passed, until it dawned on him that his intended victim was stronger than he, and that it would be prudent to break off the fight. Too late he realised that one talon was fixed firmly into bone, and try as he might he could not shake it free. Now he was totally immersed, his plumage growing more waterlogged every minute, and only his head remained above water.

The cormorant too was weakening. Blood flowed freely from his wounds, and his need to breathe was growing desperate. His leg muscles gave up the unequal struggle, and he allowed himself to be dragged to the surface. As his head broke water Iasgair went to seize him by the head, but managed instead to grasp him by the beak, twisting it and rending it so that the lower mandible was shattered beyond repair. At the same time the cormorant's frantic struggles enabled him to break free, and the two birds floundered helplessly in the water.

Luckily for Iasgair, the cormorant had unwittingly towed him into shallow water, and from there he was able to half swim, half row himself to land. The cormorant was not so fortunate. One lung was punctured, and with every breath water was drawn into his chest cavity. His beak was totally destroyed, and he would never be able to feed again. Throughout the day he lingered, half in and half out of the water, but then night came and the bite of the frost finished what Iasgair had begun. A fox found him before morning and carried his carcase away up the hill, but he left it after a few mouthfuls, abandoning it to the ravens and the carrion crows.

Although he was not physically injured, it took Iasgair most of the day to recover from the buffeting he had received, and to dry and preen his waterlogged plumage. Afterwards he was bone weary, and fell sound asleep, so when he awoke the next morning he was ravenously hungry. Fortunately the trout in the lake had recovered somewhat from their earlier harassment, and several were already sipping midges from the surface of the water. Within minutes he had dropped off his perch, and prospecting quietly over the water, he dived on his chosen victim. A few moments later he was back in his tree, a fat three quarter pounder clutched in his talons. Life at the loch had returned to normal.

The nights grew longer and colder. On the sunless slopes that faced north the line of white hoar frost advanced slowly downhill, lingering a little longer each day. Sometimes rain swept in from the north west, falling as snow on the high peaks, and though it did not lie, it was an ominous portent of more to come. The red deer stags had shed their velvet, and issued their roaring challenges from the peat bogs on the hill. Wild geese flew by, and the night echoed to the high-pitched, urgent calls of curlew as they fled south beneath the stars.

Iasgair heard the calls and felt an answering response flowing through his veins. He grew restless, and his appetite increased, so that he fed ravenously, as though in anticipation of hard times to come. Instead of resting, he spent long periods every day soaring in great circles high over the loch, as if seeking a way out from the confines of the valley. On a morning lit by the golden light of the sun and ablaze with the colours of autumn he flew south.

That night a blizzard roared in from the Arctic, spreading six inches of snow over the hills and hiding the mossy margins of the loch beneath a carpet of icy slush. By then Iasgair was fifty miles to the south, well ahead of the storm, and the wind gave speed to his wings.

Chapter Fourteen

During the next few weeks Iasgair travelled south, feeding as he went. At first his pace was hesitant, slow, as he drifted from one fishing ground to the next. Sometimes, when he found a favoured place, he lingered for days before moving on. Then one morning he would wake to feel the call pulsing in his veins, and by nightfall, when he settled to roost, he would have covered thirty, forty, fifty miles.

He caught a small pike in Bassenthwaite Lake. He took infant plaice and dabs from Morecambe Bay, gliding just above the water as the tide raced in across miles of golden sand. Although invisible when at rest, the fish betrayed themselves as they darted over the sea floor by disturbing small clouds of sediment, and Iasgair was able to snatch them from the shallow water without getting more than his feet wet.

He lingered beside a Cheshire mere for three days, fishing for roach and perch. He caught trout in a lake in North Wales, and on a broad stretch of the river Severn he snatched a chub from beneath the nose of an angler, who crouched half hidden in a gap between the willows. Later the man was able to confirm rumours among other fishermen that an eagle had been devastating fish stocks along the river.

He flew on, over the flickering fires of autumn as they blazed briefly from hill and meadow; as the russet sheen of bracken merged with the gold of birch and the paler gleam of stubble fields; and the scarlet of the maple trees shone amidst the polished bronze of the beech trees. He crossed some of the loveliest country in the British Isles, at a time when it was looking its best, yet he was impervious to its beauty.

Hunting took up little of his time. One or two fish a day were sufficient for his needs, and he seldom had to make more than half a dozen passes before he struck home and felt the savage satisfaction of his prey jerking in the grip of his talons. Afterwards, satiated, he would preen for a while before settling on his chosen perch, immobile, but not sleeping.

Throughout the day he stayed watchful, alert, ever conscious of the minutiae of movement around him. It might be a buzzard riding a thermal and winging in wide circles against the clouds; a flight of mallard streaking low over the surface of the water; a pheasant stalking slowly along the edge of a stubble field, hugging the shadow of the hedge; a tractor crawling along a lane. All was documented and filed away in his brain.

So, as the sun-drenched days of autumn grew ever shorter he drifted steadily south, across the Severn Sea and the Channel, over the green fields and forests of Brittany and France, past the Pyrenees, and down through Spain, until he came at last to the mountains bordering the Mediterranean Sea. Here a great dam had been built at the head of a gorge, holding back the waters of the river so that the valleys behind the dam were flooded with water that glowed emerald green in the sun.

The waters of the lake were used to generate electricity, and the water thus used was channelled by a series of canals to irrigate the fields in the valleys below. So, although the inhabitants of the mountains had no power to light their homes and had to transport every drop of water they needed for miles over the rough roads, the cities by the coast had ample water on tap and electric light to squander.

Pine trees grew down to the shores of the lake, harbouring herds of wild boar and deer, while the lake itself, its serpentine arms reaching out into the hills in all directions, held great shoals of carp. Over the years since the dam was built some of these carp had grown to a great weight, and seemed to spend their days basking just below the surface. They were without exception extremely wary and shy, and the slightest shadow was enough to arouse them, sending them diving down into the depths with a great swirl of their massive tails.

Fortunately for Iasgair, the greater preponderance of the shoals was made up of smaller fish, less alert, and preferring to seek safety in numbers. For the next few days he fed well, lingering beside the lake as if preparing himself for the next, and most arduous stretch of his journey.

The hunter came to the shores of the lake at dawn on the fourth day. He was a small, slight figure, barely sixteen years old, and he had already walked several miles from the road, picking his way through the trees in the half light before the dawn. He was weary, and the gun he carried, which had seemed so light when he first picked it up, now weighed heavy on his arm, while the cartridges he carried in his pocket pulled his light jacket askew, so that he was forever shrugging it back on to one shoulder.

The gun was not his. He had taken it without the owner's consent from the villa where he worked as a gardener, while his employer was absent. Indeed he had yet to fire the weapon, and since he had seen no game of any description since he had left the road, he was beginning to suspect he never would. He was understandably nervous, for he was in a hunting reserve without a licence, and while there was little chance of his being discovered, there was always the risk that the sound of a shot would bring game wardens to investigate. So he ignored the waterfowl that skated busily over the water surface below his feet, hoping instead that a stray roebuck might come down to the lakeside to drink. It had not occurred to him to wonder how he was going to get the carcase back to the road, nor how he was going to carry it home on his lightweight motorcycle.

The hours passed, and slowly the sun rose higher in the sky. Still he waited on, though he was growing hungry and thirsty and more and more discouraged. He was not aware that deep inside him lay an instinct, older than himself, older than the very civilisation of which he was a part, the instinct of the hunter, that had driven his forebears out into the chill of a primaeval dawn to face danger and hardship such as he had never known.

The sun was at its highest now, and its glare, reflected

from the water, hurt his eyes. He stood on a slight slope, the bare rock falling precipitously away into deep water, and the backs of his legs had begun to ache with the strain. Suddenly, without any warning, a large bird flew in over the trees, and cruised slowly towards him across the lake. For a moment in time it seemed to fill his whole vision, and then just as suddenly it was gone. His heart hammered against his ribcage and his legs trembled with the sudden shock and fear, and he barely had time to recover before the bird appeared again, this time flying slowly past him. Almost without conscious thought he raised the gun and fired.

The explosion was deafening in the silence. The shock of the recoil against his shoulder threw him backwards, and he thrust one foot behind him to steady himself, straight on to a small dry stick that lay on the hard rock. Next moment he was flat on his back and sliding forwards, down into the deep water at his feet. The gun flew from his grasp, clattered against the rock, and slipped silently into the lake.

A hail of shot whistled over Iasgair's head, the blast of it hurling him sideways across the sky. He felt a sudden sharp stinging pain in the small of his back, and one of his tail feathers drifted away, cut clean off by a stray pellet. Otherwise he was unharmed, and as soon as he recovered his balance he climbed high into the sky and flew off, intent on putting as much distance as possible between himself and the lake. Deep in the pine forest he came to rest in the topmost branches of a tree and settled down to preen his ruffled plumage. A bright bead of blood gleamed crimson where the other shot had lodged itself just beneath the skin.

Far away behind him the boy scrambled out of the cold waters of the lake, sobbing with fright at his ordeal. Gradually his hysteria subsided, to be replaced by a feeling of sick dread as he began to realise the consequences of losing the gun. After a while he calmed down, and crawling to the edge of the lake he peered down into the clear water. To his intense relief he spied the gun. It half rested, half hung on a ledge, the butt uppermost and about four feet below the surface. Since he was already soaking wet he slid back into the water fully clothed, and by diving down he was able, on the second attempt, to grasp the gun. An hour later he was

137

back at the road, shaking with cold, and with the prospect of an even colder ride back to his village. Still, he had retrieved the gun, and though the stock was scratched it seemed otherwise undamaged. With luck he could clean it up and put it back in the cupboard before its owner discovered it was missing, but it would be a long time before he went hunting again.

During the day Iasgair remained perched in the tree, worrying at the spot where the pellet had lodged in his back. Each time a scab formed he broke it away, causing fresh bleeding, until the feathers on his rump were sticky and matted with gore. Towards evening the offending pellet fell free, and by the time dawn broke the wound had scabbed over, and Iasgair had forgotten about it. Instead of returning to the lake he flew south, and as the sun rose he headed out across the sea, to where the distant coast of Africa beckoned.

He crossed the fertile coastal strip, and passed over the sahel, that region of scrub and cactus and thorn that marked the transition between arable land and true desert. Wandering herds of camel marked his passing, and a herd of goats scattered bleating in terror as his shadow flickered across the land. Then he was over the vast expanse of the Sahara, an interminable waste of red rock and golden sand, of shifting dunes and dreary rock strewn plains, of violent storms and whirling dust clouds, stretching for over a thousand miles. He flew the entire distance nonstop, and on the third day he reached the muddy waters of the Senegal river. Here he rested and fed, but still the lure of the south beckoned him, and after a few days he journeyed on until he reached the broad flowing waters of the Gambia.

Here mangrove forest grew down to the water's edge, the tops of the trees towering a hundred feet above the river, each with a latticework of twisted roots that curved out like prison bars along the mudbanks which were exposed at low tide. Poinsettia and tulip trees blossomed along the river banks, and tangles of creeping vines and clematis wove like lace amid the branches. The trees were alive with birds – flocks of white egrets, cormorants, ungainly storks from Europe, herons, grotesque hornbills and diminutive terns.

138

From time to time a lordly fish eagle patrolled the river, coasting over the heads of resting waterfowl. At low tide, crocodiles rested on the mudflats, and herds of hippo wallowed in the brown current.

Here too were birds already familiar to Iasgair, migrants like himself, refugees from the cold north – cuckoos, swallows and tiny, unobtrusive grass warblers. He also found numbers of his own kind, not just from Scotland, but from Norway, Sweden, and even from the Arctic wastes of Russia. Many were juveniles, still wearing the brown barred plumage of birds not long out of the nest. Some were in their second winter, having remained in the tropics all summer, and many were old birds, seasoned travellers, who had made the long flight ten, eleven, fifteen times. One osprey at least was over twenty years old.

On the incoming tide shoals of herring and mullet probed their way upriver. Although it was the dry season there was still a strong flow of fresh water, and ample feed was stirred up by the hippo in their wallowing. Here and there strange sea cows, manatees, grazed like cattle on the water weed, and they too disturbed a host of small marine insects and crustacea which fell victim to the fish.

The shoals of fish were continually harried by birds. Cormorants and diving ducks hunted them under water. Herons and storks, ibis and egrets haunted the margins, picking off those fish which ventured into shallow water, and the ospreys dropped on them from the skies. Yet the fish populations were so numerous that their legions never seemed to be diminished, and each successive tide brought fresh victims unheeding to their fate. Rarely did Iasgair need to hunt for more than twenty or thirty minutes a day. When the tide was out the ospreys moved down to the estuary, to vary their diet on flying fish, mackerel and infant bonito.

Although there was no shortage of food, there was much dispute and unseemly squabbling among the other birds, particularly the storks and herons, over roosting sites. Such disputes rarely took place among the ospreys, however, and each osprey had its favourite roost, to which it invariably returned. Fortunately, within the never-ending cycle of growth and decay in the rain forest, there were always plenty of dead trees, their bare branches standing stark against the greenery of the living mangroves. To these the ospreys returned after hunting, usually clutching a fish in the talons of their right foot, to feed and preen before settling down to survey the passing scene.

Iasgair soon located a roost which satisfied his needs. Then one morning a few days after he had arrived on the river, as he returned from fishing with a mullet flapping in his grasp, he saw that a stranger had joined him in his tree. For a moment he hovered, his plumed crest raised in anger, uncertain whether to fly on, or attack and regain his territory, but then he saw that there was in fact plenty of room for both of them.

He flew down, and settling on the branch, began to tear strips of flesh from the still quivering mullet. The stranger ignored him. Instead she just sat, slumped on the branch, eyes closed in weariness, wings drooping from sheer exhaustion. Throughout the day she remained there, as the sun rose, and the tide ebbed, and the steaming heat rose from the exposed mudbanks, bringing with it a stench of rotting meat, mud and decaying fish.

She had flown south from a land of lake and forest, where salmon spawned in the icy waters of foaming streams, where nomads still tended herds of reindeer, and brown bear and wolf still roamed the tundra. She was called Saaksi, and she was just three summers old. Her journey had been a long and wearisome toil against the weather: snow flurries over the Alps, a head wind crossing the Mediterranean, sandstorms and violent turbulence over the desert. Fortunately she was both young and in the peak of fitness, and by evening, as the tide began to flow upriver again, she was awake and alert and ready to feed. She had just time, before darkness descended over the jungle, to snatch herself a fish, and she was still tearing it apart as the moon began to rise. Then she fell asleep again, and by dawn it seemed she had taken up permanent residence in the tree.

Iasgair began first to accept, and then to look for her presence beside him in the tree, and though there seemed to be no form of communication between the two, in the months that followed a relationship developed, a bond which nothing

140

short of death could untie. So the days drifted by, days when the heat of the sun beating down on the mudbanks left the birds listless and panting, punctuated by velvet nights, redolent with the smells of spice and putrefaction.

One morning just after the turn of the year a small boy made his way cautiously along the decaying woodwork of an old jetty that leaned drunkenly out over the river. In his hand he held an empty can, around which was wrapped a length of nylon fishing line, to which was attached a hook and a small weight. Baiting his hook with a scrap of putrid fish, he uncoiled the line, and whirling it around his head he cast it out into the muddy brown water.

After only a few moments he felt a sharp tug on his line, then a series of jerks, as the fish that had taken his bait struggled to free itself from the hook. Instead of hauling his fish in, however, the boy waited, his dark eyes shining with anticipation, his white teeth gleaming against his dark skin.

He had not long to wait. A flock of terns hovered in the air over the water, and suddenly one of their number swooped down and took the fish. Then the boy laughed in wicked glee as the bird flew off, pulling his line high into the sky, while the boy played with the bird, as if flying an animated kite.

After a while the bird weakened and fluttered down into the water. The boy pulled it towards him, intending to release it, but when he had it in his grasp the tern defended itself, pecking him with its sharp bill. With a sudden scowl of anger the boy killed it by twisting its neck, and throwing the corpse into the water, he watched it drift slowly away on the tide.

Soon he was fishing again, and shortly afterwards another fish took his bait. He had let the tide carry the bait downstream, to the very limit of his length of line, but this time the terns refused to have anything to do with the hooked fish, ignoring its frantic struggles to free itself. The boy was about to haul it in when suddenly there was a rush of wings over his head. He could only watch, eyes wide and mouth agape, as Saaksi snatched the fish off the surface of the water and flew off with it in the direction of the opposite bank. The sudden jerk on the line snatched the tin from his hands, and he watched it disappear, bouncing along the surface of the water as if it had a life of its own.

Disconsolate, he climbed back off the jetty and wandered off in search of other amusement. Saaksi flew over the trees, the line still trailing behind her, until the can caught in some branches and tore the line, complete with the head of the fish, from her grasp. The sudden jolt threw her sideways, and she fell, with much ignominious flapping and screeching, into the top of the mangroves. Shaken, but otherwise unharmed, she scrambled back out and flew off to eat the remains of her catch, but the fish head, with the hook still inside it, hung down amidst the foliage. Later that day a crow found the fish head and gulped it down. As well as getting the hook stuck in its gizzard the crow got thoroughly entangled with the line, and after a while its struggles ceased. By nightfall it hung lifeless among the trees, and already the blowflies had laid their eggs on its eyes and gaping mouth.

The year was turning. Although the living was good on the river the north was calling, an irresistible stirring in the bloodstream that grew stronger with each passing day. One morning, instead of quartering the river in search of food, Iasgair headed out over the forest, across the neat fields the inhabitants cultivated on the fertile soil of the river valley, towards the dry lands of the desert. Without hesitation, Saaksi followed.

A strong wind swept them north over the Sahara, but on the second night, as they neared the coast, the south wind weakened and died, only to strengthen and veer round to the west. Ragged clouds chased the moon across the sky, and out over the sea lightning flickered and the low roll of distant thunder echoed above the waves. Dawn was still far distant, and the two birds had no option but to fly on as the gathering clouds finally extinguished the faint light of the moon.

Out over the sea the wind blew stronger, and the ospreys climbed higher in a bid to outride the storm. Now they were flying blind, and soon Iasgair lost sight of Saaksi. Tossed in the turbulence of the storm, bewildered by the buffeting of the winds and the rolling din of the thunder, Iasgair battled

142

on, but he was weary after his long flight, and the heavy burden of moisture he had accumulated from the rain and vapour that assailed him from all sides dragged him down. As dawn broke he flew just fifty feet above the waves, making little headway, his strength ebbing with every wing-beat. Just as he was about to fall headlong into the waves there loomed ahead of him the bulk of a giant oil tanker, fighting its own battle with the elements on its journey towards the straits.

Iasgair pitched down on its rolling deck and sheltered in the lee of a hatchway, wings stretched wide and mouth agape. The officer on watch marked his arrival, but paid no heed. Strange birds often hitched a ride on his vessel. They either recovered and flew away again, or they were washed overboard by the sea. Once a pigeon had ridden with them along the length of the Persian Gulf and vanished somewhere over the Arabian sea. He had no way of knowing what had become of it. Certainly he was not leaving the bridge in this weather to concern himself about the fate of one bird.

Somehow Saaksi had climbed out of the storm, breaking through the clouds into clear skies and brilliant moonlight. Beneath her the carpet of cloud, as storm-lashed and angry as the sea, boiled and fermented. Lightning still flashed, flickering rose red and yellow, but above her the stars were white. Then, miraculously, the cloud vanished, and as dawn broke she saw that she was once more over land, and beneath her lay the placid waters of a many armed lake. Gratefully she pitched down into the branches of a tall pine, and immediately fell sound asleep.

Far to the south Iasgair too slept, as the seas abated and the wind died and the oil tanker once again made steady progress towards the narrow straits of Gibraltar. Without realising it Iasgair had been blown many miles to the east by the storm. Now the tanker was unwittingly correcting the error.

He slept until it was nearly noon, before waking with a sudden lurch of fear. Without bothering to investigate his surroundings he lofted off the deck, dipping down and almost skimming the wave tops, before climbing out of danger. High in the sky, he circled the tanker once and then flew off across the sea, the sun on his back and the shoreline of Spain an indistinct blur on the horizon.

It was early evening as he flew in to the mountains, and recognised again the lake where he had once escaped death with only the loss of a single tail feather. The spring migration was well under way, and the lake was alive with birds all resting on their journey north. Several ospreys patrolled the skies above the lake, and more sat perched in the tree tops. As he approached them one of the birds roosting in the trees spread her wings and screamed a greeting, and he flew down and joined her on her perch.

Chapter Fifteen

Spring came early to Southern England that year, and as usual, when the primroses competed with the wild daffodils for their share of the sun, when the flowers of the willow gleamed fat and silver, and the hawthorn lit the drabness of a grey March day with translucent light, when the frogs in the ditches croaked all the day long, the weather was wet.

Since before Christmas the river had run high, sometimes swollen and brown, breaking over the banks and flooding the meadows, leaving behind its burden of silt to nourish the grass, sometimes, when the rain turned to snow on the high moor, flowing high and clear beneath the leafless trees. The ground was a waterlogged sponge, incapable of absorbing another single drop. Whole fields lay under water, shining mirror like under the fitful sun, and no sooner had the excesses of one downpour drained away than more rain came swirling in across the moors, driven by a moist Atlantic wind.

Nicola, housebound, had frittered away the short dark days of winter, eating and sleeping too much, regaining all the pounds she had shed the previous summer. One morning, struggling to fasten the strap of a bra that seemed unaccountably to have shrunk, she stared disgustedly at herself in the mirror. That morning she tramped six miles through the muddy lanes, and then came home and fell asleep in the bath.

Next morning her legs were so stiff she could hardly get down the stairs. Determined to punish herself to the limit, she left the house again, this time for a more modest four-mile hike, and thereafter it became a daily ritual. Unable to do anything in the garden, she turned the spare bedroom into a makeshift gym, and worked out a mixed programme of callisthenics, yoga, Swedish drill and weightlifting that occupied her for an hour each day. She cut down on gin and cigarettes, and ate less starchy food, until her bra fitted comfortably again, and her jeans were positively baggy around her waist.

There came a morning in March when the weather gods relented, and soon after dawn the clouds parted to reveal a sky as blue as a thrush's egg, and a land lit by a yellow sun. Since the garden was still too wet to work on, Nicola busied herself removing some of the dust and cobwebs revealed by the inquisitive sunlight that peered into corners hitherto dark and forgotten. Soon wearying of this, she made herself some coffee, and afterwards grabbed her jacket and set off down to the river.

Though the sun was warm the wind off the moor was cool and fresh on her cheeks, and she zipped up her jacket and strode along briskly, enjoying the morning, and her new found fitness, which made walking a pleasure. The river wound before her, now lying like a broad ribbon of black and silver between the water meadows, now hidden in a clump of willow and alder from which chaffinches sang and blue tits quarrelled. Hazel catkins danced in the breeze, and from somewhere in the distance came the low roll of a woodpecker.

She spied the lone angler while she was some distance away, and at first she thought it was Martin. For a moment her heart beat faster, and she was immediately angry with herself for reacting in that way. Sternly she reminded herself that the affair was over, and that she had no further interest in the man. She hesitated, about to turn back, but then she decided that if she gave him a wide enough berth he probably wouldn't even see her.

Then as she drew nearer she realised the angler was a stranger, casting a dry fly upstream for trout. Despite herself she was captivated by the grace and skill of the art, the line lazily curving out, and then straightening just above the water so that the fly landed on the surface as delicately as thistledown. Then, as she watched, a dimple appeared on the surface of the water, and the wand-like rod bent in a bow. A few moments later a fat golden trout slid into the waiting landing net, was despatched, and slipped into the old fashioned wicker creel the angler carried on his back. Then she was past him, and apart from noticing he was elderly, with a thick mane of silver hair, she paid him no further heed, relieved to see that he was too engrossed in drying his waterlogged fly to be aware of her presence.

She walked on a while, until she reached the old humpbacked bridge that spanned the river, still called Newbridge, although it was almost two hundred years old. Here she paused, wondering whether to take the long way home through the lanes, or turn back the way she had come. She sat down on a fallen log, left by the winter floods, and turned her face to the sun. Seeing the angler had unsettled her, reminding her of Martin, and the loneliness of the past few months. Not for the first time she wished that the visit to Scotland could have ended differently.

Worst of all was the nagging feeling that all she had to do was to call Martin, and their relationship would be just as it was before. Paul had told her that Martin always asked about her whenever he visited the trout fishery. He was doing well, enjoying such popularity among the angling fraternity that he had to turn away clients, but he seemed reluctant to make friends, remaining aloof and reclusive, even declining to join Mary and Paul for a meal. Paul was, Nicola knew, unashamedly matchmaking and Mary was worse, asking her if she had seen him every time they met.

She was hungry for companionship, hungry for a purpose in life, hungry for love. Right now she was hungry for a ham sandwich, a big thick one, with mustard, and perhaps a beer to wash it down with. She set off back along the river, walking briskly. At one point she started to jog, and then remembered the angler and slowed down again to a walk. She was dimly aware of shouting in the distance, a sound reminiscent of a football match, or children let out of school, and she wondered what it could be.

A group of teenagers stood by the river, boys and girls, all dressed in anoraks and jeans. Some wore woollen hats with bobbles on them. Others were bareheaded, but at least two wore balaclavas pulled down to hide their features. They were throwing sticks and branches into the river, wading out as far as their wellington boots would allow them and beating the surface of the water.

Even as she tried to figure out a reason for their strange behaviour she saw the old angler, standing in the middle of the stream, still holding his rod, but no longer fishing. Instead he stood, head bowed, shoulders hunched, making no attempt to remonstrate with his persecutors or to leave the stream. He looked for all the world like a beaten dog. It was then she remembered his age and began to run.

She had suddenly realised what the pantomime was all about. She had heard of so called 'antis', self styled activists protesting against blood sports, but she had never seen them in action before, and though she had heard of them protesting against anglers, she had assumed that their energies were directed mostly against fox hunters. Now she knew differently.

She didn't see who threw the stone. She only saw it strike the old man on the side of the head, so that he staggered and almost fell, holding one hand to his head as the blood ran down his temple and over his face. She let out a bellow of rage and began to run faster. The group had already seen the result of their actions, and had checked their unruly behaviour in sudden fear and awe. The sight of Nicola running towards them was enough to make them panic, and they scattered at her approach, ignoring her pleas, threats and demands for help. In a remarkably short space of time they had vanished, and Nicola was wading out into the stream towards the angler, who stood dazed and bewildered, as if unsure where he was, or how to get back to the bank.

Gently she escorted him to the river bank and sat him down, fumbling in her pocket for a handkerchief. To her chagrin she had only one paper tissue and a small lace edged handkerchief, unfortunately exceedingly grubby. She folded the tissue into a pad and placed it over the wound, but it was of little use.

The man's face was very white, but after a moment he stopped trembling, and to Nicola's surprise his eyes began to sparkle with secret amusement. 'Never thought I'd become a scapegoat,' he murmured. 'I thought that behaviour was confined to Biblical lands.'

'Please,' said Nicola. 'My home's not far away. Come with me, and I'll put a dressing on that wound, and make you a coffee. Better still, a large scotch. If you can walk, that is?'

The old man nodded, and after a moment got shakily to his feet. 'I'm fine now, I think. More insulted than injured.'

They set off back along the river, Nicola carrying the old man's rod and creel. They had to pause to rest several times. Nicola could see the old man was shakier than he was prepared to admit, but at last they reached the cottage, and she sat him down in a chair while she went to change out of her wet jeans and then get warm water, antiseptic and adhesive dressings.

When she returned the angler had taken off his jacket, and to her surprise he wore a clerical collar. 'Oh!' she stammered. 'I beg your pardon.'

'For what?' queried the stranger. 'Oh! this. My flea collar. Don't let it bother you. I had an early communion to take this morning, but when I saw what sort of a day the Lord had sent us, I felt it would be churlish of me to waste a minute of it. So I set off down the river without bothering to change. Permit me to introduce myself. Adam Roscoe, C of E. From Dorset, actually, but standing in for your local man while he undergoes some essential repair or other.'

Nicola introduced herself as she bathed the wound caused by the stone. The bleeding had stopped, but the parson's temple had begun to swell, and he had the makings of an ugly bruise. 'I don't think you'll need stitching,' she said, 'but I'm no expert on these matters. Would you like me to run you down to the casualty department?'

'Heavens no, child, thank you all the same.' The mischievous twinkle came again into his eye. 'I'd have to forego that scotch you promised me.'

'First things first,' murmured Nicola, applying a dressing, and washing the rest of the blood off his cheek. Then she poured her patient a large drink, wondering the while whether it was approved medical practice, and then on reflection pouring one for herself. Once they were settled comfortably, she looked at him over her glass. 'We ought to notify the police,' she observed.

'We ought, I agree,' said Adam. 'But would it serve any useful purpose? We don't know who these miscreants are, nor where they came from. They'll spend the next twenty-four hours blaming each other, and wondering whether retribution is about to fall on them, and by then maybe they'll have been punished enough.'

'It's more likely that by then they'll have recovered their nerve and will be back again harassing someone else,' retorted Nicola. 'Still, as you say, it would probably be a waste of time. Let's compromise. I'll have a word with my neighbour, and he can tip off the river bailiff. He can step up his patrols, and call for assistance if need be.'

'Agreed,' said Adam. 'Certainly other anglers ought to be aware of the situation. Strange, isn't it, how often people can use high moral principles to justify violent action?'

'Have they got high moral principles?' queried Nicola. 'Or are they just bored teenagers looking for an excuse to stir up trouble?'

'Oh, I'm sure that you are right, but I'm equally sure that many individuals experience real anguish at the thought of inflicting unnecessary suffering on other forms of life. The trouble is they conveniently forget the teaching in the Sermon on the Mount. You know, that bit which says, "Why beholdest thou the mote that is in thy brother's eye, but considerest not the beam that is in thine own eye?" if I've quoted it correctly.

'It always amuses me to see, when young people protest about something, they always wear tee-shirts and jeans. Yet the production of cotton has, in terms of pesticides, herbicides and destruction of natural habitat, been more devastating to wild life than a fullscale war. I couldn't help noticing your kitchen garden as we came in. Soon, no doubt, you'll be getting it ready for spring planting. Yet I suspect that if the Lord had it to himself for any length of time, he'd do away with all your neat rows, and fill the garden with what people used to call vermin – moles and pigeons and rabbits and deer – and probably put a blight on your broad beans. The caterpillars would have a field day. Yet any good gardener must destroy legions of God's creatures every time he wields a hoe. And all because he enjoys fresh fruit and vegetables. But then, if I were to stage a protest against young ladies wearing jeans, or gardeners spraying their fruit trees, I too would be forgetting the teachings of our Lord.'

He drained his glass and bent to pick up his creel, which lay on the floor beside his chair. 'Look,' he said, and opened the creel.

Three fat trout lay on a bed of green fern, their flanks golden, the row of red spots down their sides glowing against the mottled green and olive of their backs. 'Was there ever a more beautiful example of God's creation,' he murmured. 'Yet I have had the temerity to take their lives.'

He closed the lid of the creel. 'If you quote me as having said this I'll deny it, of course. I tried to be a dutiful servant this morning and administered the sacrament with all due reverence, yet I confess my mind was on the river. I only hope that when I eat these fish it will be a form of sacrament in itself, one I shall undertake again with reverence, as well as a good appetite.'

He chuckled to himself. 'You know, as a kid I used to have to say grace. Before every meal I had to fold my hands, bow my head, and say "We thank thee lord for this our food but more because of Jesus's blood may manna to our souls be given the bread of life sent down from heaven amen." Just like that, without a pause for breath, and I didn't understand a word, or even think about what I was saying. Yet I wish today, instead of saying grace, children were taught to pause a moment before meals, just to reflect on where their food had come from, and the sacrifices that had been made, of all living creatures, just so we might eat.'

He set the creel down again on the floor. 'I'm sorry my dear, I'm preaching. It is my job, I suppose, but I really shouldn't inflict my whimsies on the converted. Especially since I suspect I still haven't justified my killing a fish. I could just as well make do with a sausage.'

Nicola laughed. 'Speaking of which,' she said. 'It's past lunchtime. Will you join me?'

The old man jumped to his feet in dismay, and then had to grab the back of the chair for support. 'Good Heavens, my dear, I wouldn't dream of imposing. I'm sure you have had quite enough of a garrulous old man for one day. I must thank you for all you've done. A good Samaritan indeed, and a feisty one at that.'

'Please,' said Nicola. 'I wouldn't have asked you if I wasn't enjoying your company, and I think you ought to rest a while longer.'

Adam hesitated, and then, 'Well, only if you share my catch. There's ample for two. I was going to give a couple to my housekeeper, but I have a feeling you would appreciate them more.'

There was a bottle of white wine in the fridge, and the makings of a salad. Adam took over the cleaning of the trout while Nicola put a splash more whisky in their glasses and set about preparing the salad. Before long they were chattering and joking away like old friends. It's true what they say, thought Nicola. The Lord does move in mysterious ways. But she didn't tell Adam. Instead she asked, 'Why flea collar?'

'A little girl came up to me one day and asked me if I'd got fleas, and when I asked her why she wondered that, she said her cat wore a flea collar exactly like mine. I asked her if her cat had fleas, and she said, "No, not as long as he wears his collar." So I said I was the same. Though sometimes, I feel, people do look at me as though I have them.'

Lunch was delicious, and prolonged. In the beginning Adam had done most of the talking, but gradually, as the level in the wine bottle dropped, Nicola found herself telling him more and more of her story, beginning with the sudden death of her husband. 'And that,' she finished wistfully, 'is where I am at the moment, just drifting, not knowing what I want, neither happy nor sad, but just ... dissatisfied.'

Adam set down his glass and laid his hand on hers. Afterwards Nicola was tempted to blame it on the wine she had drunk, but it seemed to her at that moment that from being a mischievous imp, her companion had suddenly acquired an air of authority. Yet when he spoke, his voice was hesitant, gentle, almost apologetic.

'Forgive an old man's presumption, my dear, but would I

be right in suggesting that your late husband was a man of high principle?'

Nicola nodded.

'Not perfect,' Adam continued. 'None of us can lay claim to perfection in this life, but shall we say he was what people these days refer to as politically correct. And would it be true to say that at times he was not the easiest of men to live with?'

Nicola nodded again.

'And now it seems to me that you are seeking perfection again, or at least your idea of it. You need to ask yourself whether you want this man as he is, or as clay that you can mould to your own desire. But let me warn you again. You will not find perfection in this life, no matter how far you look. We're back to the Sermon on the Mount again, aren't we? Judge not, that ye be not judged. Of course, you're entirely free to reject our Lord's teachings. It's quite fashionable these days. But whatever their merit, at the very least I find they knit together to form a fairly cosy sort of security blanket.'

He took his hand away from hers, and the old twinkle reappeared. 'Don't underestimate the power of missionaries, my child, and think long and hard before you become one yourself. When the early Jesuit Fathers went out to convert the heathen Eskimos to Christ one of them asked, "If you had not come and told us about the Saviour and the blessed Mary the virgin, would we have all gone to hell?" "Of course not," said the Jesuits. "Then why did you bother?" asked the Eskimo. The point, I feel, is not that the Jesuits bothered to spread the word of the Lord, but that the Eskimos were prepared to listen, and to accept their teachings.

'As a small boy I was got at by a clergyman. I had won a prize for some trivial essay on natural history, and when he heard about it he presented me with a copy of a book, *Wild Life In a Southern County*, by a nineteenth century writer and naturalist, Richard Jefferies. I've since read all his works, and his views, on field sports and conservation, long before the term was even coined, have influenced me ever since. I believe they should be required reading for all sportsmen and environmentalists alike. You should try them. But now I've

153

talked enough. You've plied me with so much good wine I expect I've talked more nonsense than usual.'

'I'll make some coffee,' said Nicola hurriedly, and escaped to the kitchen. Unaccountably, she was crying, and she could not for the life of her think why. She only knew she was conscious of a deep feeling of relief, of demons exorcised from her system. When she returned with the coffee, the reverend Adam Roscoe was sprawled in an easy chair, sound asleep.'

Chapter Sixteen

Far to the north, MacDonald had just finished building a nest, or rather the foundations of one. He had read that in many regions, particularly in the United States, osprey had been encouraged to settle by providing artificial nests in suitable sites. These were particularly inviting to young ospreys, which when nesting for the first time took so long building their nest that there was no time left in the season to breed. Then they had to wait another year. By giving them a helping hand, it was possible to help them breed younger.

Some of these nests were truly artificial, even taking the form of old packing cases and wagon wheels, but MacDonald felt that for the island site something more natural and aesthetically pleasing was called for. Taking advantage of a window in the weather, he drove his old Landrover as far as he could, and then skied over the hill to the loch. The waters were still frozen hard, and with infinite care he crossed the ice over to the island. Once there, he cut down a couple of small pine trees, carefully choosing two which were stunted and misshapen, and growing too close to other trees. He trimmed the branches to three-foot lengths and then tied them in a bundle to the end of a rope, the other end of which he attached to his belt. Then he turned his attention to the tree he knew was favoured by the osprey as a roost.

Scorning the use of climbing irons, which would damage the trunk of the tree, he took from his rucksack several stout lengths of cord, to which he had tied short wooden blocks. Reaching round the bole of the tree, he tied the loose end of the cord to the block. He fastened the next block about two feet up the trunk, on the opposite side of the tree. Then he fixed another, thus creating a series of steps on which he stood as he worked his way slowly and methodically up the tree. It was painstaking and dangerous, for if a cord should break or a knot slip he could fall and lie injured and broken on the island until the frost brought an end to his pain, but all went well, and soon he reached the lower branches of the tree, from where the climb to the crown was relatively easy.

Hauling up his load of branches, he proceeded to weave and lash them into a secure platform about two feet in diameter, using tough green nylon cord he hoped would be strong enough to withstand the gales. This took him most of the morning, and then he had to descend for a second load. He took a break to eat a quick lunch of soup and bread, looked regretfully at his whisky flask before returning it unopened to his rucksack, and then climbed back into the tree. He had to work fast if he was to finish his task and still have time to ski back to his vehicle before darkness fell and he was benighted on the mountain.

As a final test he climbed into the structure and sat down heavily, rocking to and fro and looking for signs of weakness. His lashings held, and though the cradle groaned and squeaked as the branches rubbed together, it did not fall. Satisfied, he descended the tree, untying his climbing blocks as he went, so leaving no trace of his activities. His last task was to cut the few remaining branches from the trees he had just felled and scatter them around in the hope the ospreys would carry them up to the nest themselves. The trunks he rolled away into the undergrowth. From the ground the structure certainly resembled a half-finished nest, and Mac-Donald crossed the icy lake once more then set off back up the hillside, weary but satisfied, hoping the ospreys would be impressed with his handiwork.

It was fortunate that he had chosen that particular day, for by early the next morning a blizzard began to blow, and for three days it snowed hard. Then a rapid thaw set in. The first signs of spring appeared in the shelter of the glens, which echoed to the bubbling call of the curlew and the peewit's plaintiff wail, but up on the hills winter still reigned, and everyone knew it could return to the lowlands at any time during the next few weeks. Yet already the osprey were arriving back on their breeding grounds. MacDonald heard of two pairs, old and experienced birds, which had already returned and begun work on their nests. He fretted impatiently, anxious to see if his bird had returned, and whether he had acquired a mate, but until the weather improved and the snow drifts melted on the hill he had little chance of making his way over there.

Spring came earlier to the sheltered Devon coombes, and throughout the day Martin's trout fishery was loud with birdsong, relayed against the low, companionable chorus of rooks busy at their nest sites. Already the black caps and willow warblers had arrived from Africa to join the resident songbirds. Sand martins skimmed the surface of the lake, mallard and coot nested in the reeds, and the Canada geese returned. As the last sleepy quarrelling of the blackbirds on the wooded hillside died away a nightingale flooded the night with song.

There was in addition a continuous procession of birds in the sky overhead: curlews on their way from the estuary to the high moors, their urgent piping calls repeated at regular intervals; herons with slow, graceful wing beats that belied their speed; cormorants on urgent business of their own. Throughout the day Martin observed the traffic, from the moment he woke and took the first look out of his bedroom window, to last light. He even took to carrying his binoculars during the day, after he spotted what he felt certain was a Montague's harrier, which was flying too high for him to be absolutely sure.

A pair of buzzards regularly nested in the woodlands high on the slopes of the coombe, and Martin grew accustomed to their daily appearance as they flew in wide circles prospecting their territory for prey, or rode the thermals rising from the valley. So when, one morning, he paused in the act of dressing to look out of the window, he barely gave the two large birds circling over the lake a second glance. Then, as he turned away, something about them made him look again. They were too large for buzzards. The wings were too slender, too long, and then, as the rising sun lit them from underneath, he saw the white underparts, and the pronounced black wrists on the wings. Ospreys were once again visiting his trout fishery.

His elation at the sight of them was mingled with dismay at the thought of what it was going to cost him to feed his guests. Were they planning to take up residence for the summer, build a nest and raise young, or were they migrant birds just resting on their way north? It was at that moment that it occurred to him that one of the birds might be the one Nicola had rescued, now returning with a mate. If this was indeed the case one of the birds, at least, should be ringed. He looked around for his binoculars, remembered he had left them on the hall table, and ran downstairs, still in his bare feet.

He stepped outside, gasping at the shock of the icy dew on his toes, and anxiously scanned the air. One of the birds, he thought, was wearing a red ring, but he was looking into the sun, and he couldn't be sure. He moved quietly round the side of the house, hoping to find a better angle of view, but at that moment a party of anglers drove up to the gate, and both birds vanished over the trees.

Cursing, Martin went back inside the house and slammed the door. Some anglers were just too keen for his liking, and although he flatly refused to unlock the padlock on the gate before eight o'clock in the morning, there was nothing he could do to stop them arriving half an hour, or in this case almost an hour early. As usual, he ignored them, and while they assembled their tackle, drank coffee and gossiped among themselves he finished dressing and cooked his breakfast.

He consoled himself with the thought that it was just as well if the ospreys moved on. Despite this he found himself anxious for the day to end, for the anglers to go home, in the hope that when all was quiet the birds would return before dark. Throughout the day he kept scanning the sky, and as soon as the fishermen had departed he locked the gate and hurried inside the house to resume his vigil beside the bedroom window.

An hour passed. Slowly the sun sank behind the shoulder of the hill. Soon it would be too dark for the ospreys to hunt. Then, just as he was about to abandon his watch, both birds

158

flew out of the woods and began hovering over the lake. As he watched, one of them dropped on a fish, talons wide and legs outstretched, and at the moment before it hit the water he saw quite clearly that it was wearing a red ring. Bearing the fish in one talon, it flew off, but the other lingered, prospecting over the water until it too succeeded in catching a trout. Martin winced at the size of the fish he had lost, and then shrugged. Thoughtfully, he went downstairs to prepare himself a meal.

All day he had promised himself that if the ospreys did appear again, he would telephone Nicola and invite her over to see them. He was sure that she would be unable to resist the chance of seeing her protégé again. Yet now the time had come he still hesitated, terrified that he might receive yet another snub. Memories of their visit to Scotland still alternately delighted and haunted him, and despite their differences, he knew that he would like nothing better than to be her partner for life. Yet he was determined that it would be a partnership. He refused to be dominated, or persuaded by any form of emotional blackmail to give up a pastime in which he could see no wrong.

Several times during the next hour his hand strayed towards the phone, but each time he checked himself. He was looking at it for the fifth time when it started to ring, making him jump almost out of his skin. To his utter astonishment it was Nicola herself, phoning to tell him about the assault on the minister, and to warn him, because she was afraid he might run the same risk of personal injury. 'They might even try to sabotage your home, or the lakes,' she concluded. 'So I felt you ought to know.'

Martin was so delighted to hear her voice that he scarcely bothered to pay attention to her warning, but he did take in enough of what she was saying to understand that she too might have been in some danger. Nicola assured him she had not come to any harm, and she could sense the relief in his voice as he thanked her for taking the trouble to call. Then he asked, 'Would you like some good news?'

She listened with mounting interest as he told her about the return of the ospreys, and when he told her about the red ring she was suddenly certain that one of the pair was the bird she had come to regard as hers. 'I thought you might like to come over,' he ended, as casually as he knew how. 'They may not linger more than a day or two.'

For a moment she did not answer. Part of her wanted to say yes. The other recoiled in panic. Her conversation with Adam Roscoe had given her a lot to think about, and after he had left, acutely embarrassed at having fallen asleep in her chair, she had sat for a long time in a state of confusion and bewilderment. She could either dismiss his little homily as rubbish, which it patently was not, or accept it, which meant that two people with totally opposing views could be equally right, or wrong.

In the end she had given up trying to resolve the paradox. Right now, all she wanted to do was to see Martin, and the ospreys, again. Almost without realising it she heard herself agreeing to drive over to the fishery by first light the next morning, and as she put the phone down she realised she was trembling.

Martin replaced the receiver and sat back in his chair, a broad smile of satisfaction on his face. 'How to lure a girl to your lair,' he murmured to himself. 'Invite her to see your fish hawks! Oh well, it's original at any rate.'

He was too restless to read or watch television, so he took a stroll round the lakes, enjoying the mild spring night and the scent of countless plants and herbs. Around him he could hear faint rustlings and stirrings, the stealthy movements of small creatures going about their affairs. By the margin of one of the lakes frogs croaked in concourse, and somewhere in the distance a nightingale was tuning up for his night's performance. A soft wind blew from the south. There would be no frost that night, but Martin hoped the wind wouldn't get too rough. Too much disturbance on the lakes would put the fish down, and then the ospreys might not appear.

He turned in early, anxious to be ready and waiting when his guest arrived, but for once sleep eluded him. He tossed and turned on a bed unaccountably full of lumps, turned on the light and tried to read, but could not concentrate. He put the book aside and turned off the light, preferring to lie in the darkness and let memories of Nicola come flooding back. Nicola rosy-cheeked and breathless, muffled against

160

the cold, Nicola sleek and sophisticated, in high heels and stockings, not beautiful in the accepted sense, but breathtakingly attractive, with that wide mouth and those strange amber eyes.

Such recollections were a luxury he had hardly dared allow himself until now. They did not help to induce slumber, but eventually he must have dropped into a doze, because when he next opened his eyes his bedside clock registered the time as just after three am. Something had disturbed him, he didn't know what, but then he heard the sudden clamour of the Canada geese by the lake. It must have been their cries which had awakened him.

He knew that ever since the days of ancient Rome geese had been highly prized as watchdogs, being far more reliable than dogs when it came to giving warning of intruders. He wondered briefly what could have disturbed them, a fox probably, but then he remembered Nicola's warning. Was someone out there, threatening to sabotage his fishery? He slipped out of bed and padded over to the window.

There was a small moon low in the sky, and the wind was gusting, driving small clouds over the face of the moon, so that the night was alternately bright and dark, with shifting shadows playing across the landscape, shadows that seemed to move along the margins of the lake. For the first time Martin wished he had gone to the expense of installing security lights. It occurred to him that if someone wished to damage the fishery beyond economic repair, seemingly without causing harm to the trout, then all they had to do was to open the sluice gates that connected the lakes, and let water and fish drain away downstream to the main river. That the alien fish might not survive long, or if they did could seriously disturb the ecology of the river itself, would not occur to them.

There was nothing for it but to get dressed and take a look around. Without putting on the bedroom light he pulled on slacks and a sweater, and slipped into a pair of moccasins. He stepped out of the front door, collecting a stout ash plant that stood in a corner of the porch, and moved silently down towards the lakes.

He had not bothered to take a torch, knowing that it

161

would betray his presence to any intruder. He preferred to rely on the light of the moon, and his sense of smell and hearing. All seemed quiet. He doubled back to the gate to check the padlock and peered down the lane in case a vehicle was parked there, but there was nothing. Then it occurred to him that anyone planning to interfere with the sluices would open the bottom one first, and he headed back to the lakes. He waited, listening, until a cloud darkened the moon, and then crept silently across the grass.

Faint silver light flooded the valley for a moment and then was gone, but in that instant he was sure he saw a shadow where there should have been none. Moving swiftly now, he darted forward, his ash plant firmly grasped in his right hand. The shadow took substance and shape, a white face turned towards him, and he heard a warning shout. Instinctively, Martin lashed out, his ash plant connecting hard with what felt like solid flesh and bone, and he heard a bellow of rage and anguish. At that moment, as he reached out to deal the intruder a second, more telling blow, his foot slipped in something soft and slimy, his injured leg gave way, and as he lurched forward, he felt something thud into the side of his head. His last thought, as he fell face down on the wet grass, was that Nicola would be arriving soon and there would be no one to open the gate.

Nicola too had passed a restless night, and long before dawn she was up and dressing, searching her wardrobe for garments that would be attractive as well as warm. At last she was satisfied that she was at least halfway presentable, but even then, as she stepped out of the front door into the chill of the morning air, it was still only the half light that precedes the dawn. Even the birds were silent. The dawn chorus had yet to begin, and only a blackbird seemed wide enough awake to utter a few sleepy notes. So she dawdled along the lanes, the car heater full on and the window wide open, enjoying the smells and sights of spring and prolonging the delicious sense of anticipation for the moment when she would arrive at the gate and see Martin waiting to greet her.

Only he wasn't. She switched off the ignition and sat for a moment, listening to the engine ticking as it cooled. Then she got out of the car and walked to the gate. It was still firmly padlocked. The dawn chorus was in full swing now, and the lakes were flooded with light, but Martin was nowhere in view. She felt an initial pang of disappointment, and then a mischievous grin crept over her face. The lazy bones was still in bed. She would go and throw stones at his window.

She walked round the corner of the house, and almost fell over him. He lay on the front doorstep, one leg drawn under him, one arm outstretched towards the door as if he had been trying to get into the house, the other arm cradling his head. A dark mat of blood and hair disfigured his head above his left ear, and the blood had run down over his face and down his neck, so she couldn't see how badly he was hurt.

She didn't need to check his pulse. He was breathing, but in a snoring, stertorous way that frightened her, and she knew she had to get help. Fortunately the door was unlocked, and it opened inwards so she didn't have to pull him out of the way. Stepping over him she went inside and found the telephone. She called the ambulance, and they responded straight away, but she knew it would take them twenty minutes or more to negotiate the narrow lanes. Meantime she was at a loss to know what to do.

She couldn't move him, and she dared not do so, even if she had the strength. She could only cover him with blankets in an endeavour to keep him warm. Fortunately the bleeding seemed to have stopped, and she didn't think he had lost a serious amount of blood. It then occurred to her to find his keys, to open the gate, and move her car out of the way so that the ambulance could get through. Even so it seemed an age, though in truth it was only a few more minutes, before she heard the siren and saw the blue light twinkling towards her through the trees.

The ambulance men were efficient and kind, but they shook their heads sadly when she asked if they thought his skull was fractured. 'Have to wait for the X-rays, dear. Can never tell with an injury like this.'

They asked if she could tell them what had happened, but she knew no more than they did. After they had gone she lingered awhile, uncertain what to do next. She guessed that in a short while anglers would be arriving, but she hadn't the vaguest notion what Martin's duties were, nor even what he charged his clients. Reason told her that there was little point in racing after the ambulance. It would be some while before the doctors made their diagnosis. On the other hand she desperately wanted to be at Martin's side when he recovered consciousness.

This last desire won. The anglers would just have to be disappointed for a day or so. Still, she forced herself to make a cup of coffee, and as she sipped it scalding hot she prowled restlessly around the room. Her eye fell upon a bookcase, and idly she ran her eye over the list of titles. The same name on several volumes caught her eye, that of Richard Jefferies, and smiling at the coincidence she picked one out at random. It was a small slim volume entitled *Life In The Fields*, and seemed to be a collection of essays, or articles culled from magazines. On impulse, she slipped it into her pocket before she locked up and left the house.

There was good news and bad at the hospital. Martin's skull wasn't fractured, but he had not yet regained consciousness. There were fears that a blood clot might be pressing on his brain, and an operation might be necessary. Meantime he was resting in a private ward, and she was welcome to sit with him as long as she wished.

They had cleaned the blood away from his face and neck, and fortunately his breathing had returned to near normal. Nicola sat down and took his hand, but it was cold and unresponsive in her grip. Nevertheless she held on, and after a while she remembered the book she had brought with her, and drew it from her pocket.

She found it hard to believe that the words she was reading had been written more than a century before. Ideas and beliefs that she thought peculiar to her time, and a supposedly enlightened era of so-called environmentalism, were clearly familiar to the author. In one essay he deplored the commercialism of shooting and the wholesale slaughter of predators for the protection of game, yet acknowledged the shelter provided by copses, coverts and marshes for species which would otherwise be driven out by arable farming and the spread of urban areas. By his own admission he himself was never happier than when he was roaming the fields with a gun, yet he made passionate pleas for the preservation of what was considered then to be vermin.

Though he did not appear to enjoy hunting so much, still he recognised its role in the countryside. 'Without the protection that hunting affords them, foxes would certainly have disappeared. The stag and fallow deer are other examples.' Clearly he disapproved of otter hunting, but drew a distinction between control of otters, and their extermination, as was apparently already happening on the Thames.

In a delightful essay on the water-colley, or dipper, he extolled the joys of angling, even when the river was low and conditions were poor. 'Experience and reason were all against the attempt, yet so delightful is the mere motion and delicate touch of the fly line on the water that I could not but let myself enjoy that at least . . .' But the fish were small, '. . . to destroy these undersized fish was not sport . . .' so he watched the dipper instead. 'It is the birds and other creatures peculiar to the water that render fly fishing so pleasant; were they all destroyed, and nothing left but the mere fish, one might as well stand and fish in a stone cattle trough. I hope all true lovers of sport will assist in preserving rather than in killing them.'

Throughout all his writing his authority lay not in academic awards, nor in scientific training, but in his descriptions of every minute detail, and vivid accounts of country matters, showing that from the time he could walk he had been a patient and accurate observer of all that went on around him. As she read, Nicola found herself wondering why she had never come across his work before. Then another thought struck her, one that she would once have considered disloyal. Had David known him? It seemed highly likely, but then why had he never mentioned his works, or commented on them? Perhaps he had thought it simpler to dismiss his writings than try to integrate them with his philosophy.

An hour passed, and then two. From time to time she paused in her reading to watch Martin's face, hoping to see some sign of returning consciousness there. Her eyes had just returned to the open book in her lap when she felt the slightest pressure on her hand. She looked up and Martin's eyes were open. 'Hi,' he said.

A long time afterwards she realised she had forgotten all about the ospreys.

Chapter Seventeen

A thousand feet above the loch, Iasgair soared in wide circles through the cloudless sky, a still quivering trout grasped firmly in his talons. Beneath him on the eyrie Saaksi watched as he swept by high above her. Gradually the circles grew narrower. His call, a high-pitched piping cry, echoed across the mountains as he drew nearer to the nest. Above her he climbed higher, a hundred feet, two hundred, three, then hovering briefly he spread his tail in a wide fan and dived, dropping like a meteor with the fish outstretched before him.

At the last moment, just when it seemed he was about to crash on to the nest, he powered skywards once more, only to repeat the whole performance, calling all the while, his cries growing more urgent and ecstatic. Again he swooped skywards and dropped, this time plummeting down in a long dive which carried him straight on to the nest. Gravely, Saaksi accepted the fish, and Iasgair flew off to find another branch to add to the growing pile.

They had been back at the nest site just over a week, and already the eyrie was nearing completion. Iasgair had soon exhausted the supply of sticks left by MacDonald, and had culled most of the other dead sticks on the island. Now he was forced to range further afield, sometimes journeying several miles in search of a good source of material. Meantime Saaksi was busy decorating the nest, lining it with smaller twigs, moss, heather, dead leaves and withered grasses. More dangerously, she also brought remnants of plastic, strips of rag, and discarded lengths of bailer twine, which could entangle the feet of the young birds later in the season.

Not until she was satisfied with her domestic arrangements would Saaksi submit to Iasgair's ardour, which grew more urgent and demanding with every gift of fish, but there came a day when, instead of snatching the offering and flying off to her favourite feeding perch, she stayed on the eyrie, tail raised, wings outstretched and quivering. Then Iasgair mounted her, and with much flapping of wings, and scrambling about on the platform, they consummated their desire. Thereafter they mated frequently, gradually gaining more skill in the process, until one day at the beginning of May a single brown egg lay in the eyrie. Two days later there was another, and Saaksi began to brood in earnest.

As soon as MacDonald knew that the pair had settled on the nest site he hastened to inform Nicola. Rather than telephone Martin, Nicola decided to go over and see him, and give him the good news in person. He was making a slow but steady recovery from his injury, and was, he insisted, quite capable of looking after himself once more. He was still weak, however, and tired easily, so Nicola found herself spending more and more time at the trout fishery.

Often in May the temperature drops as the sun goes down, and clear skies are an omen of frost by the morning, but this particular evening a warm wind blew from the south, bearing with it the scent of the wild hyacinths which flooded down the wooded hillsides and lay in a purple mist under the trees. It needed but an hour to sunset, and Nicola expected to find Martin resting, or watching television. She was somewhat taken aback to find him preparing his fishing tackle, assembling his rod and reel and checking through the pockets of his fishing waistcoat.

He had the grace to look guilty at being caught out. 'The sea trout are running,' he growled. 'I'm tired of staying in all evening. I'm going to have an hour by the river.'

He expected Nicola to object, but he was disappointed. 'Why not, if you feel fit enough? It will do you good.' She hesitated a moment. 'Can I come?'

Martin regarded her keenly for a moment, and then nodded. 'Sure. I expect you'll find it a bit boring in the dark. You won't be able to see anything that's happening.' It never occurred to him that this was exactly what Nicola wanted.

This way she could accustom herself to the idea of angling, without having to watch the fish suffer. It was, she was prepared to admit to herself, a fairly feeble and spineless reaction, but she saw no reason why she should make life hard for herself. She grabbed a thick sweater and a pair of gumboots from out of her car, and climbed in alongside Martin. On the way to the river she told him about the osprey. He seemed pleased, but made no comment.

The sun had sunk behind the hill, but still the light lingered as they sat on a log beside the river. Slowly the sleepy chinking of the blackbirds died away. A woodpigeon flew in on a busy clatter of wings and pitched noisily in a tree above their heads. Somewhere a dog barked in the distance, and a few minutes later a fox ambled by on the opposite bank, so intent on his own affairs that he failed to notice them sitting quietly side by side.

A sea trout rolled heavily under the bank on the far side, the sudden hollow splash startling Nicola so much she jumped. Beside her Martin chuckled. 'Don't worry,' he said. 'It does that to me too. You never get used to it.'

'When do you start?' she asked.

Martin laughed again. 'When there are seven stars in the sky. When you have seen three bats fly past. When you can t stand the waiting any longer, like now. He stood up and made his way down to the water's edge. Nicola could hear him stripping line off the reel, and then the soothing hiss of his line running through the rod rings as he began to cast. She stayed sitting on her log as he moved slowly down the pool and the dusk swallowed him up.

Now that she was alone the night seemed to take on new dimensions. The trees and bushes seemed to crowd closer, as if to inspect this alien in their midst. Somewhere an owl called, and suddenly the song of the river seemed to grow louder, as if calling her to its edge. She shivered and huddled deeper into her sweater. It would be easy, she thought, to let images of monsters and the ghosts of drowned fishermen crowd into her imagination. Resolutely, she put such thoughts from her mind, and wondered instead what the ospreys were doing.

A sudden shout and a flurry of splashing roused her from

her reverie. A bar of silver erupted from the pool, and Nicola heard the screech of the reel and a clattering of loose stones as Martin ran upstream towards her, reeling frantically as he came. A few more minutes and it was all over. The fish leapt three more times, ran back down the pool, and then settled to fight in slow circles, until, after the manner of its kind, it gave up all resistance and slid on its side to the waiting net. Martin tapped it on the head and switched on his torch. 'Three pounds if it is an ounce,' he murmured with satisfaction.

He came and sat down beside her on the log. 'I think that's enough excitement for one night,' he remarked. 'I'm still shaking at the knees.'

To her surprise Nicola felt reluctant to leave. She wanted to sit on, cloaked in the velvet stillness of the night. She realised that, robbed of the sense of sight, all her other senses – of hearing, smell, and even touch – were heightened, made more perceptive. She couldn't remember when she had felt more alive. She turned to look at Martin. He was regarding her intently, his face a pale blur, the pupils of his eyes unnaturally enlarged against the white. Quite slowly and deliberately he kissed her, and as she sank into his embrace it was if she was drowning, so that after a few moments she broke away gasping. A moment later she was back in his arms again, and it was as if all their differences were washed away, carried off into the night by the river flowing by their feet.

Some time later Nicola struggled to her feet. 'Home!' she said firmly. 'I thought you said you'd had enough excitement for one night.'

Reluctantly Martin stood up. 'Allright,' he said. 'I'll make you a cup of cocoa, or something.'

'Or something!' Nicola agreed.

They settled instead for scotch, and Nicola found the bottle and glasses while Martin weighed his fish. 'Three pounds two ounces,' he announced as he laid it on a dish. Nicola went into the kitchen to admire it as it lay there, deep of flank and small of head, pure silver merging to the faintest hint of gold, darkening almost to black. The spots too were black instead of red, and Nicola found it hard to believe it was one and the same family as the brown trout Adam

Roscoe had caught. A few tiny crab like creatures clustered near the tail, and as she stared at them one moved. 'Ugh! she exclaimed. 'What are those?'

'Sea lice,' Martin told her. 'They drop off after a few days in the river. Shows the fish is just in from the sea. You'd better come to dinner. There's too much fish there for one.'

They took their drinks through and sat side by side on the sofa. Suddenly they were both shy and ill at ease. At last Nicola set down her glass. 'Its getting late,' she murmured. 'I'd better be on my way.'

Martin held out his hand. 'Don't go,' he said simply.

Nicola looked at the outstretched hand and then took it in hers. 'Come on,' she said, and led him upstairs to the waiting bed.

If the party of anglers who arrived early the next morning was surprised to see Martin strolling hand in hand with a very attractive woman along the edge of the lake they were too polite to say anything. The Canada geese, floating on the calm surface of the water regarded them warily as they approached, and the gander let out a low hiss. 'Dratted birds,' said Martin ruefully. 'It was one of their droppings I skidded on that night when I was attacked. Still, falling like that when I did may have softened the force of the blow just enough to have saved me from a fractured skull.'

'The police have got the man they think attacked you, haven't they?' asked Nicola.

'That's right,' said Martin. 'A guy called Ernie Snell. His mate brought him into casualty with a broken jaw and a lacerated ear, the same morning as I was there.'

'You must have hit him hard,' she commented.

'I meant to,' replied Martin grimly. 'He's rubbish. Nothing to do with the anti-blood sports brigade. He's well known as a poacher hereabouts. He's also wanted for a whole series of crimes – vehicle theft, assault and battery, and burglary. I gather they've been after him for some time, but they've never been able to pin anything on to him before. Now, hopefully, he'll be out of circulation for some time. All the same, I've got security lights fitted now.'

171

They wandered on a while, until they came to the sluice at the end of the bottom lake. They rested a moment, leaning on the rail of the little bridge over the outlet stream, the exact spot where Martin was attacked. 'There's something I'll never know,' said Martin. 'How I got back to the house from here.'

'It's as well you did,' said Nicola with a shudder. 'I might not have found you, and gone away not realising you were lying down here hurt.'

'As it was, you missed seeing the ospreys,' said Martin. 'I've been wondering. Would you care to go back north? See them on their home ground so to speak?' He hesitated a moment. 'I promise not to go salmon fishing while we are there.'

Nicola laughed sheepishly. 'I'd love to go. But you go salmon fishing if you want to. I'm sure I could find something else to do. I've been thinking, actually. I'd quite like to learn how to fish the fly for trout, and I certainly enjoyed last night. Maybe you could teach me. It's just that salmon fishing is a bit too much for me.'

They set off back to the house together, making plans for the proposed trip.

It was early June before they could leave, and since there was no urgency to travel fast they drifted slowly north, avoiding the motorways. Instead they followed the old roads, passing through towns and villages, exploring winding roads that led from one enchantment to the next. At night they stayed at wayside inns – the only enduring landmarks, save perhaps the churches, left in the land – Martin flaunting his plastic cards and refusing to worry about the dent he was making in his bank balance.

Their journey became a litany of rivers – Exe and Severn and Wye and Dee, Weaver and Ribble, Lune, Eden and Esk – majestic rivers with musical names, rivers older than the fields and woods around them, that had served mankind since he first explored barefoot along their banks. Once they had been worshipped, worthy of human sacrifice. Down through the ages they had served as highways and sources of power. They had been used and abused, obstructed, drained,

172

polluted and defiled. Now, as a source of recreation and pleasure, they were growing once more to be loved.

This was the season when they were looking their loveliest, their banks clothed in the fresh green of early summer, their waters clear and cold. Martin could never resist stopping for a closer look, and to speculate on the quality of the fishing they provided. Finally he said, 'If we stop and stare over one more bridge, the birds will have flown back south before we get there.'

'Mm!' said Nicola dreamily, making no move to tear herself away. 'It's just that I want this journey to last for ever. We could always go to Africa.'

'We could do that, I suppose,' said Martin. 'In the winter, when we are sick of the English weather.'

At last they went back to the car. 'A river is a very hard thing to tear yourself away from,' said Nicola. 'I'd hate to live anywhere very far from one.'

They stayed once more at the small hotel where they had spent the first night of their previous visit. The stag's head was still on the wall, but there was no haggis on the menu. Instead, they settled for a steak and kidney pie, which was at least solid and substantial enough to render them incapable of movement for some time. They retired early, for they had arranged to meet MacDonald the next morning.

The sun shone from a cloudless sky, baking the hillside as they set off once more towards the loch, vainly trying to emulate MacDonald's effortless stride. 'I'm thinking the eggs are just about to hatch,' he said. 'So we'll need to be careful not to disturb the parents. If they both start calling we must come away at once.' Martin merely grunted. Unlike MacDonald, he could not climb hills and talk at the same time.

Their guide led them to a small outcrop of rock where they could lie in the sun and be sheltered from the thin, cold wind that blew down from the snowfields still lying in the sunless hollows of the hills. For a long while nothing happened. They could just make out the head of the brooding bird sitting on the nest, but of her mate there was no sign. Then suddenly he appeared, seemingly out of nowhere, cruising lazily high in the air over the loch.

173

As they watched, he hovered briefly and dived, disappearing in a silver shower of spray. Next moment he surfaced, a fat trout flapping wildly in one claw. Instead of bearing it to the nest, he flew with it to another tree on the island, and proceeded leisurely to tear the flesh from around the head.

Half an hour passed. The osprey fed from time to time, pausing for long periods to stare around him at the sky. At last, when he had consumed about half the fish, his mate began to call, a nagging, peevish, high-pitched cry. As if remembering his duty the other bird picked up the remaining half of the fish, flew to the eyrie, and presented it. His mate snatched it from his grasp and promptly flew off the nest, carrying her meal off into another tree. The other bird watched her go, and then very gingerly settled himself in her place.

The long day passed. After she had finished her meal the female spent some time attending to her toilet, meticulously preening her plumage and arranging each feather neatly in place. Then she took off for a short flight, returning with a spray of green pine needles, which she wove into the nesting material before taking over her duties as a mother.

At last, stiff and cramped, the watchers crept out of concealment and made their way back down the hill. As they did so the male osprey flew low over the heather. At the sight of them he climbed skyward, and then checking himself, circled low over Nicola's head. Three times he swooped past her, before flying away back to the loch. Ever after, Nicola was to wonder whether he had recognised her, and whether it was his way of thanking her, and of bidding her farewell.

Next morning they headed south once more. Towards the end of the first day they made a detour into the Lake District, home, as Martin remarked, of Wordsworth and John Peel. They stayed at a small hotel appropriately called The Fish, lying between two of Lakeland's loveliest lakes. That evening, at dusk, as they walked by the shores of Buttermere, Martin asked Nicola to be his wife. 'I've got no ring,' he confessed. 'I didn't dare presume that far, but I can think of no one I'd rather spend the rest of my life with. I'd like to marry you, if you are prepared to make that commitment.'

'With all my heart,' said Nicola, and then she laughed softly. 'And I know just the man to perform the ceremony. An ancient Dorset pixie, who had the good sense to appear just when he was most needed.'

Much later that night, Nicola was awakened by moonlight streaming in through the bedroom window. She got out of bed and looked out. A silver pathway lay stretched across the length of the lake. The hills were dark against an indigo blue sky, and the feathery tops of the pines stirred in the small breeze. Through the stillness came the soft murmur of the stream that flowed between the two lakes, and in her fancy it seemed to whisper a prayer to the earth as it hurried on its way. A phrase came into her head: 'A river is a lifetime long.'

She wasn't sure what it meant, or even if she'd heard it before, but it was a strangely comforting thought to carry her on her way.